The Sound of Living Things

The SOUND of LIVING THINGS

ᏖᏖ *Élise Turcotte* ᏖᏖ

TRANSLATED *by*
SHEILA FISCHMAN

COACH HOUSE PRESS
TORONTO

Coach House Press
50 Prince Arthur Avenue, Suite 107
Toronto, Canada M5R 1B5

FIRST EDITION
Printed in Canada

Published with the assistance of the Canada Council,
the Department of Communications, the Ontario Arts
Council and the Ontario Publishing Centre.

Canadian Cataloguing in Publication Data
Turcotte, Elise
[Bruit des choses vivantes. English]
The Sound of Living Things
Translation of: Le bruit des choses vivantes.
ISBN 0-88910-437-9
I. Title. II. Title: Bruit des choses vivantes. English.
PS8589.U62B713 1993   C843'.54   C93-094709-6
PQ3919.2.T87B713 1993

For Clara and Francis.
Thanks to them there is at least one
life for each thing.

And for Alain.

Images

A number of things happen in this world. Sometimes they are contained within a dramatic event or a happy one, or simply in the condition of one's surroundings. A woman desires a man, the sky turns black, a tree falls, struck by lightning, there is a war, a refugee camp, a crying child. Some people feel their hearts beating too fast, others will never exist. The baby who was born in Iran just after Christmas, for instance. I remember it well, it was bitterly cold and Maria's gifts were all over the house. What I mean is that, here, things really do exist. The TV image was very clear: a baby with two heads, one torso, two hearts, two sets of lungs. What was most surprising was that one head was asleep while the other was crying. I immediately thought about a woman who has just killed her husband. She is motionless, you can sense that stillness everywhere: it insinuates itself into every room in the house. The woman is sitting on the sofa, one eye weeping, the other wide open and dry. I got up to look in on Maria, who was asleep. I thought again: cruelty isn't what we think.

Images, that's what I'm getting at. We are all very busy people, for images never leave us. Some of us can occasionally switch off everything in our heads. Not me. Images accumulate in my brain alongside the numerous corridors I must take to get myself out of there. I open a door, I walk down the corridor, and here I am outside, in front of a store window, looking at a sparkling piece of jewellery. Sometimes I go inside and put the piece on a credit card: then I wear it as proof of my lightness. But all the images are still with me. I spend hours poring over the dictionary, I want everything to have a meaning, I want everything finally to hold together and one thing to be present within me, something quiet and full, and that thing would be life. I can't do it. I can't even think great thoughts like everybody else, I can't do anything, all the little things in life are spread out before me. At night I see baby's pajamas, I shift furniture, I make amends for something I shouldn't have done. I know very well that the baby's pajamas have been placed in my brain on top of something more foolish. And in the end I'm always afraid.

The woman who killed her husband—it was in a movie—suspected nothing, only afterwards was she able to make this incredible statement: "I finally know what it is to lose your head. This instant is mine. I am free." Her image is always present in me. Alongside it are the little Iranian baby and Maria, with her plaid dress, white socks, white collar, her extraordinary smile.

2

Fortunately, time is there to put everything in order. When I'm frightened I know that the night will pass: I close my eyes, the night passes ... And so when Maria was born, I told myself over and over that it was only a matter of time: I counted the hours, it couldn't go on past a certain number of hours.

And then the hours vanished with the pain and I was left with Maria.

We were both so white, and there were strange high-lights on our skin. Maria was already my whole life, but I was well aware that I mustn't be that to her. Not forever, at any rate. That's what I've always found hardest about love: not to be someone's entire life.

Maria is three years old now. I'm thirty, my name is Albanie, and I live alone with my little daughter. It is thanks to her that the things around me exist.

An example of something that exists: the clock on the table by my bed really exists, its alarm goes off, its hands are white, they move and the numbers have a thousand stories to tell.

Other examples: the pink sky, the crayon that coloured it pink, doorknobs that are always falling off, square cats.

Every day, Maria calls me on the phone. Even though I'm right there beside her. For Maria, I am the person who is there. I am the present tense. I can never die because I am the present. But Maria is never sure of anything. From morning to night she says over and over: Mummy's there! Is Mummy there?

On the phone, she calls me by my name. In pho-tographs I am always Albanie. And when we make a huge cake out of sand, we both sing, very softly, Happy Birthday to Albanie.

That makes me a character in Maria's life. A living object who conveys an image of reality. A being who is sometimes inside another being, sometimes outside.

What Maria likes: shapes on her bed-sheets, books, fashion magazines, lollipops, jewellery, drawing, singing into a microphone, making a calendar.

What she doesn't like: dogs, the slide she fell off yesterday, parrot shows, children who cry at daycare, noise,
loud singing, applause, shouting.

One night she hides her head under the comforter and
says, I'm scared. Her little nameless fear again.

I close my eyes, find myself completely in what she
says.

It's all right, Maria, it's just the wind, it's the wind
blowing at the window.

The wind?

For Maria this ushers in a kind of delight. A thousand
times, she says she's afraid of the wind. It is her object.
Fear becomes a goal, a source of joy, for Maria.

Or everything can be divided into seasons or geometric shapes, or into castles, oceans, houses, forests. They are
Maria's theatre. At the entrance to the forest there is no
danger. You can count the trees, you can even find a little
clearing to pitch your tent. There you will dream of something abstract, of a colour moving across the sky. And
then all these things can become characters. Nothing is
abandoned. The characters are covered with jewels, they
have brothers or sisters, they have friends. Some of them
cry, others break things. Occasionally one of them will
lose someone, and then we must do all we can to find him.
We must offer consolation for everything.

For Maria, it's a question of entering into the very
essence of words. Each one contains different stages, all of
them bridges to be crossed. It is never-ending, for we are
on a continent of words.

At the end of one of these bridges I sometimes catch a
glimpse of Maria. Her head is down, she is following our

progress into the sea. I am with her. Around us, on the boat, some people are writing letters, others are closing their eyes and thinking of what they will say to the person with them. We are far from the house. Perhaps we've finally managed to lose a little of what we left behind. Phrases occur to us, we don't retain them: they fly away out to sea.

3

There are mornings when Maria can make me forget what time it is. I forget about work, the library, her daycare, I forget almost everything except what Maria calls the real things. She says that, the real things. She goes to the living room to watch "Ramona" and calls me when there's an important scene. And that's how we dismantle what remains of the night. After breakfast, we smear citrus cream on ourselves so we'll smell of grapefruit: that scent always makes us feel suntanned. Then when we're really ready, we can get dressed and go out.

At the library today I have to shelve a series of cookbooks in alphabetical order. The food of China, of Japan, the Seychelles Islands, Madagascar. I keep looking at the clock above Madame Raymond's head. Ten o'clock: Maria is watching "Tales of the Green Forest." Two o'clock: she's doing arts and crafts, she's drawing another square cat. Grandma is sitting on the sofa, reading the paper. Now and then she closes her eyes: she is organizing her thoughts. Then she puts the paper on the table and looks at Maria for a long time. She sits her on her lap, congratulates her on her drawing. She slips it into a big envelope and writes on it: For Mummy Albanie. Three o'clock: now I am shelving novels in the B section. Belleto, Brontë,

Boyd. No. Belleto, Boyd, Brontë. After every ten books or so I go over to the Ms where three days ago I started to read *The Member of the Wedding*. I'm not making much progress in either the shelving or my reading. There's no need to say what Madame Raymond thinks of me.

At the end of the afternoon I go to the "New Arrivals" section to borrow the latest book by Dr. Brazelton. Jeanne and I have read almost all of them. We talk about them on the phone, we say Brazelton says this or that, he has never fallen asleep beside his little daughter, he's never done something that can't be mended. This book is about the family and work. Just the thing for us.

I put the book in my bag, I take Madame Catastrophe, Monsieur Étourdi and Madame Risette for Maria. Madame Raymond doesn't say, Goodnight, Albanie, but I go out smiling anyway, I'm thinking about my child, about the evening we'll spend together.

Supper time: a circus, as usual. But bath time goes smoothly because of the fish in the tub with Maria. Maria adores fish. There is a moonfish, a ray, a shark, a whale. Her father brings them to her.

Later, just after story time, I fall asleep beside her. I wake up feeling guilty, I call Jeanne to tell her. Adding that I'm sure Dr. Brazelton's wife doesn't work and doesn't have to do everything by herself the way we do. Jeanne says that once again she's too tired to watch the news. I go back to sleep in my own bed. I think: this has been another day, Albanie's and Maria's day. If we look closely, it means that the space in which Maria and I are two is beginning to endure. It must endure in our heads and in our dreams, for it is there that everything will begin to stir.

4

We've just seen some pictures of hurricane Hugo. Another of the things that happen in this world. There is more confusion here than there was in the picture of the Iranian baby, but less madness than in the eyes of the woman who killed her husband. But pictures don't tell the whole story about the things that happen. That's why Maria and I always add our private conclusion to any collective drama.

It's raining. Maria is rebuilding the houses that have been destroyed while I, sitting beside her, am trying to convince myself that nothing is a sign of anything. Dreams are not signs of death, five good years are not a sign of seven bad ones, coincidences don't point to me or to anyone else. Joys are joys, and sorrows, sorrows.

It's not that.

I just have to think about that time when in one brief moment everything became, inevitably, a sign for something else. A bookmark inserted into a book upside down, a forgotten deed, a child's story. When Maria's father left.

At first, time was taken over by a kind of light. And then by space. Finally, by acts that were no longer merely acts. Words opened up, allowing other words to fall.

In her own way, Maria understood perfectly well what was going on. She saw Mummy crying and Albanie always on the phone. At night I thought about her endlessly, with no brother or sister, and most of all there was my dreadful fear of losing her.

That's still my greatest fear, it fills my dreams. Because I do dream, but my dreams are not signs of the future.

I wanted at least one sister or brother for Maria, so that childhood and everything that goes with it would settle into the house anarchically and for a long time. I wanted my love for her to be spread around a little.

But things didn't work out that way. The two of us are alone and my love for her is strong, too strong.

Images of Albanie's fear.

Perhaps the first is the story of the hidden shoes. First image of loss: I was five or six, I don't remember. The shoes were black patent leather, the most beautiful ones I'd ever seen. My first big-girl's shoes. Besides, they were shiny. I never wore them.

My mother and I had stowed them in the closet by the front door where they were very visible, and they shone even in the dark. The next day, though, no more shoes. And most important: no one ever figured out what could have happened.

Shoes have now become an emblem of desire. And desire contains the fear that is the emblem of disappearance.

Other images of loss, later, as I held my child in my arms. At the top of the stairs: a false move, I trip and tumble down, the child, so small, falls, the earth stops turning. Or this: posters bearing the pictures and names of missing children. Insane ideas about what has happened to them, about how they died: kidnapped; raped; diseased; abandoned. Or again: it could be Maria, the baby who choked to death, the missing baby could be Maria.

In the depths of my love there is always that precipice, a hidden land where Maria is taken from me. Deeper still, there are all the children and most unimaginable of all, the suffering of children.

Maria has rebuilt an entire city. I am building a tower around her, I put bars on its window.

Every morsel of our life is an event. Everything is a sign of everything.

I create a portrait of Albanie: she opens her eyes, she breathes, she holds her purse very tight in her arms, she thinks, I don't want to die without something in my arms; she tells someone over and over, don't go, please, please, don't go away.

5

Once upon a time there was a pink balloon and a wood-pecker pecked it and the balloon burst. That's the story, Mummy. And now the balloon's going to cry.

Maria says, That's the whole story: things break and then they cry. She puts her pencil on the little white table, she just remembered that I won't be home tonight. This is the night when Jeanne and I go out. Stamping her feet, Maria says again that she wants to come with us.

When Jeanne arrives Maria tells her right away, she doesn't like secrets whispered in her ear.

Jeanne unwraps a little treasure for Maria: a marzipan crocodile.

Come here, Maria. Come and pick out Mummy's jew-ellery.

I'm wearing jeans and a black sweater and as usual when I go out, I wait and put on lipstick at the very last minute. For kisses. As soon as the baby-sitter crosses the threshold, the lipstick can go on. Maria thinks I'm beauti-ful, too beautiful to be going out.

But Jeanne is already waiting outside. I go down the stairs and don't turn back. I check to see that my keys are in my purse. There's a trace of my love on Maria's cheek.

At the bar.

There is a murmur of things around me, bottles, the mirror, I can't hear what Jeanne is saying, my bracelet is talking, I don't know how to be present here.

It's always the same: all the girls are taller than I am. Some of them have red hair and amazing dresses. Their voices are next to their mannerisms, flat on the table. Their mothers aren't watching them from a distance. Or their children. And I, there's always something that kills me.

I can picture myself very clearly, with my cowboy boots and what no one sees, the western movie in my head. Every night at least one person comes through the saloon doors of the bar, and every night I turn and smile into the line of light, even more alone although there are people all around me. But nothing shows.

Jeanne nudges me with her elbow because someone has just taken the chair beside us. I mean, right beside me. A man. He's looking at me too much.

An hour and several drinks later, I tell him to stop, stop looking at me, I talk very formally, like Maria when she's playing doctor or when she goes into a jewellery store; then I kiss him with my mouth and everything around it, suddenly.

He of course thinks it's the truth or something like that.

Jeanne laughs hysterically.

I put on my serious face and again I kiss him as if we were being shipwrecked.

Later, too late, I hear myself telling the man two or three final little things. Love is a sickness. I also talk about what Maria calls the shapes of life. Mountains, the sea, boxes, clocks, joy, windows. I say, You see, that's what we are on this earth.

When I think he knows everything about me, when everything ends up truly wrecked because of the alcohol, it's time to go home.

I know now how to recognize that moment. The end of an evening can very well resemble the start of a love affair, but it's never that. We are only beginning to be someone else. Another woman, another man. Someone who has been left but is no longer suffering. Or the reverse. Someone who has not been left, but is suffering still. Or both at once.

In the taxi, Jeanne laughs again at my taste for strangers.

I tell her, It's been like that ever since I was born.

Is Maria asleep?

Is she breathing?

Is she caught in a bad dream?

6

The man from the bar has called. His name is Alexandre. A name I hate, but he's handsome, tall the way I like them, black hair, which I also like, and so on. Like Maria's father.

A date for dinner.

A date after work at the library.

Finally, a date at my house, late, very late, so Maria will be fast asleep with the angels.

It's the third day and he undoes my belt. The space inside the house suddenly shrinks, we are in my bedroom, we're going at it in earnest, especially me, I'm pulling his hair. I feel good because for once the things around me are silent. Except perhaps the picture in the book beside my bed. It shows a road and it's quite clear that we are on that road. There's a sky with clouds descending, it seems as if the grass on either side of the road is yellow, and on the right there are three trees with the same foliage and a little house. The soil is arid and all we hear is the sound of the wind. It's also the sound of a life that's continuing, somewhere else, but still it continues.

I make love by the side of that road, I am still alone, and on the fifth day Alexandre still doesn't understand why I can't sleep with him. But I can't. I'm still just as alone by the side of that road.

I know it won't work out, I mean I do everything to prevent it from working out. I get up in the morning hoping to find a love letter in my shoes. But I never do. At night the road stretches out before me, I must go there, I must take that road, I must feel uneasy with my little suitcase on the ground at my feet.

This story doesn't belong to me.

I tell Alexandre.

I also tell him that I'm not myself, that I hear another voice when I say his name, that perhaps we drank too much on all those evenings, but now I'm tired, and in my fatigue I feel too remote from myself and from Maria.

So goodbye.

Thank you.

Let's leave things as they are, let them be stamped on us to see if they will produce a great love that erases everything else. Even sorrow. Even wounds that have never healed.

7

At the end of the week, Jeanne turns up with Gabriel one evening. It's rare for us to go a week without seeing each other. But my time was filled up by Alexandre. And by the past. And by Maria.

It's autumn now, there are apples all over the house, pies, apple sauce, drawings of apples. We explain what trees do, and the difference between sweet and salty. Maria asks what's the difference between mummies. We laugh, especially Gabriel, who at five thinks he's much more grown-up than Maria.

Jeanne.

Above all she wants to know what happened with Alexandre. She lures me into one corner of the kitchen. I don't know the answer.

She thinks my affairs never have any follow-up. That's true. What I like, what I've always liked, are beginnings, every beginning of every love affair.

At the library at lunch-hour sometimes, I'll choose let's say Section A, and I'll read the first sentence of every novel there. Then a world is awakened for me, a whole world in a single row of books.

Very well. We talk. That's something Jeanne and I do well together. For instance, we're always a little excited by the theme: Is life a novel? In the end we invariably discover one tremendous difference: in real life we often enter a love affair in the middle. That's why it takes so long for things to start. And I'm not a very patient person.

Neither is Jeanne, for that matter. I let her talk, not saying anything: she spent all summer working on her house. She didn't know that she'd done that, but I did.

She said, Something has to happen, something has to start moving. She began by washing all the windows to let in the light, the sky, words from the street. Then the walls. And all the rest. Even what was hidden in closets and cupboards. She kept that up for two months, the two best months of the year. She wasn't smiling in the morning when the light rose over her little crystal ball. She soaped her finger to remove her diamond ring and she went on. Then, when summer was over, she realized what she'd done. She prepared a more elaborate meal than usual. Fish, white wine. They ate slowly, she and Jacques, because Gabriel was with his father. Then she told him to leave. That was all. Just like that.

Now Jeanne asks me again if she should keep the diamond. I say yes. Because it's the most precious stone of all. It's not part of Jacques's body or his gaze. Barely a memory.

Diamonds are forever and we decide to make them the symbol of her new life.

As far as Alexandre and I are concerned, still no answer.

8

When Maria runs in to tell us there are lots of candies on the shores of the Nile, we forget our stories and all four of us are in Egypt, inside one of theirs. I'm glad, because there are a lot of things I like today: Maria's questions, apples, Jeanne's diamond, Gabriel's winks, and geography.

I am content.

But at night, because joy and sorrow are sharing the same space, after Jeanne and Gabriel have gone, after Maria has fallen asleep, fear returns to take another stitch on my vocal cords.

It begins with spiders, at least one in every room, and

in my bedroom there is a little white cocoon, empty, in the corner by the window.

I kill them, every one. Except of course the one with the empty house. I don't know where she is. I look for an hour at least, it's late, and if I don't get to sleep right away I'll never sleep again.

It's done. I didn't go to bed and the spider is still suspended above my head. Jeanne is right, there's never any follow-up to my love affairs. I don't have flowered sheets or a spotless silk nightgown. I'm not someone who lets herself make only those remarks, smile only those smiles that are necessary, who falls asleep as soon as her head touches the pillow.

I think about the subject of purses that are the same colour as shoes. Here it is: a woman sits in a café, taking tidy little sips of espresso, she is calmly leafing through a newspaper, really concentrating: this is no act she's putting on. She's had eight hours' sleep, she got up for breakfast, she donned a brand-new dress and just by chance she found in her closet the perfect shoes and the perfect matching purse. She never snoops in the papers of the man she lives with. She doesn't lie down on her child's bed and feel lost because the child isn't there. She thinks about her work, and that justifies her existence. It's justified because she controls the flow of her words and her deeds. One of her friends shows up and sits beside her, she is a sieve, a magnet who attracts anything that can leave traces. She hasn't slept, she can't say why. Something wrong with her brain. She listened to the song by Sting after her friends left, on the video-clip she saw all the Argentinian grandmothers holding aloft placards with pictures of their disappeared grandchildren. Born in prison, perhaps dead in prison too. She also saw Enrique, who still has his mother's picture over his heart, and, closer to here, little Felix who doesn't speak, who walks past the house and never raises his head. She doesn't know how she can continue with that. To leave everything outside herself. She has got rid of the spiders, she has closed some doors and opened others, she has listened to the breathing of her child. Now she looks at the woman and she wants so much to be like her, with her perfect clothes and every hair in place.

A memory now. I'm sleeping with someone who is madly in love with me, who is going to leave his wife for me and who will go back to her two weeks later like a beaten dog. Anyway, that was long before Maria was born. I was working at another library. I didn't look like much, but my white blouse was unbuttoned at just the right place. The man, who was peering hard at me, thought I was terribly sensual, and I think I really was. Because it was summer and all that. The shutters swayed in the wind and at night they cast a forlorn light on the floor. I mean, the wind came through the window and brought with it a sadness, and I didn't know where it had come from. That was why he fell in love with me. The white blouse, the shutters, the sadness. Those things loved us, language loved us, but our desire was more loving than love itself.

I had got up in the night to try to learn more about the ghosts in the house. I had opened the doors of all the closets and cupboards. Everything was so neat and tidy. There was a place for each category of object, you could never make a mistake. Clothes. His wife's in the closet on the left, his in the closet on the right. The little basket on top held underwear, folded in a way I'd never seen. Then, sweaters. One basket for wool, another for cotton. And then scarves, belts, stockings. All of it carefully separated. The shoes lined up like schoolchildren. All staring at me, and even at night I was like a stain on the wall. I suddenly understood that what he desired about me would never get the upper hand.

That night, the drawers and the clothing were signs, a kind of nightmare on top of other nightmares. It came, of course, from love. Or rather from a desire to be loved properly.

To be loved properly, that is to be bowled over by the other's desire.

Three a.m.: too late to call Jeanne now, too late for the last movie on TV.

I cling to time. I close my eyes, the night passes.

Tomorrow will be a normal day, with anxiety and loss buried at the back of the garden. We will put on our aprons, Maria and I, and we will be extraordinary. In the park we'll build a sand-castle that holds every form of life. For a moment the sky will bend down into our eyes and nothing will ever come between us and the world.

9

I am barely awake and already I hear Maria playing doctor. A very noisy game. Everything is in place, she has created a system for each category of medicine. She says, Here, this is for the children's mummy. She speaks very politely. You can call somebody else. This is all done, of course, on the telephone. On the telephone you speak properly, and very politely.

Today, Saturday, is a day off. For Maria, a day without daycare or Grandma. It's our day. Tomorrow too.

We decide to work hard in the house because it's cold outside. We make a list of things to be done:

1. Bake a chocolate cake.

2. Call Jeanne and Gabriel to come and sample our cake.

3. Console Jeanne if she is sad.

4. Make up a story and write it out on sheets of paper folded in half like a real book.

5. Make a drawing for the cover of the book. Think up a title.

6. Draw a planet for Daddy who will come to pick up Maria tomorrow afternoon.

The story begins badly: a little girl gets her fingers cut off by her mummy. She meant just to cut her nails, but she got distracted and the next thing you know a finger has been cut off. Maria says she read this story in the newspaper. Finally there are two little girls, Julie and Stéphanie, they like candy but not candles, like Maria, they draw a forest and then get lost in it. Their parents find them and it's night, in the country.

Maria draws an owl on the cover. The owl is black, the night blue.

Later, Alexandre calls, he'd like us to try again. He's lonely.

Right away, the road lined with yellow grass. Trees. Their foliage.

I talk a lot. I say no, I don't think so. I tell him a story: this summer, a little boy drowned in the pool. A public pool. The adult had told a four-year-old to keep an eye on his eighteen-month-old brother. He falls into the pool. No one sees him. For a moment, he is so small through all the arms and legs, the swirling water, the voices that are more and more remote. Then, the colour of his skin. His limp body, so small. People find him. They shout. We know it's all our fault.

And then the road again, the wind.

Alexandre doesn't want to hear stories like that. He sells houses, he doesn't read the papers, he's lonely. In the evening he goes to see shows, he has a drink, comes home, slips between the sheets, and sleeps. Or he meets a girl like me. He says, like Albanie. He wants to be the one who will make her forget everything—the road, drowned children. And Maria?

I don't know how to say no. When I hang up, we've agreed to get together tomorrow. Sunday. While Maria is with her father.

10

Jeanne and Gabriel have come to sample our cake and now Maria talks about daycare. She tells us there's someone there she doesn't like. Someone, we don't know who it is. At first she thinks it's me. She says, I don't like Mummy. She refuses to get dressed, to eat, to do up her coat. Every morning, on daycare days, everything comes undone, nothing holds together.

Maria tells us this: she stays in the cloakroom for a long time and when the children's shouting becomes too loud she goes away. She walks along the corridors, it's an old school. She goes to another classroom, she knows that behind the door is Lise, whom she likes. She opens the door and Lise picks her up and holds her. When I come for her, her cheeks are still puffy, just under the eyes.

So that's it, even on weekends Maria is afraid of falling

asleep. She thinks the nights are too long. How can we know where we will wake up tomorrow, how can we be sure nothing will have disappeared? How can we know if we should hide so that we can watch the bees and planets die?

The night-light has been lit. Images on the floor, spread out around the bed.

Maria explains something else: the Eskimos make a huge snowball and throw it up to the stars. And so the Eskimos are drawn to the stars.

She falls asleep.

In the living room, Jeanne is waiting for me to resume our conversation. She tells me again that there will never be another follow-up to a love affair. Not for you, she adds, and not for me. She thinks that it may be because of the children. She isn't sad. She's thinking.

Gabriel is asleep on my bed with his shoes on.

Maria is dreaming: whenever she turns over, we hear the little bell on the cat she's holding tightly in her arms.

The plates will stay on the table all night.

Jeanne, stretched out on the sofa.

Gabriel and Maria asleep.

I am in the black chair, running my fingers through my hair, seeing an image of Maria that I don't want to see.

It seems as if another little apocalypse is beginning.

11

Maria's father.

In the past you could say: Albanie is fine, Albanie is happy. She's not feeling anxious, she is breathing the warm afternoon air, the curtains are open, she's not alone. She has Maria and Maria's father. In the morning, two little hands overwhelm her with joy. At night she is able to talk; even better, a man takes her in his arms, breathes in the smell of her neck, pushes back the silence of the house.

One day he is no longer there. And then everything has to be explained. I mean, for Maria's sake I must pretend that I understand. That's all. There's nothing else. Albanie knows how to put things back where they belong.

Sunday.

When he arrives I open the door, I see the yellow leaves carpeting the ground.

Maria is hiding under the sofa cushions. He looks for her everywhere, in cupboards, behind doors, he makes a sobbing sound and then there is the spectacle of finding Maria.

Bursts of laughter, kisses.

I go to the bedroom, I come back with a little pink suitcase full of clothes. The suitcase barely shuts, because in addition to her clothes there are the indispensable familiar objects—the little cat with the bell, the red alarm clock, books, crayons.

And then the spectacle of going away. Now Maria doesn't want to leave, she wants Daddy but she doesn't want to leave. She wants things to form a whole. Her crayons, her scribbles, her drawings, and time enough to finish everything. Just one way of being rocked to sleep, just one house.

The open door, the carpet of yellow leaves.

We have tricks in our bag, we say sly words, Maria climbs into the car, finally she smiles.

I turn around, I don't like anything about what has

just happened. I pick up the toys in Maria's room. I do use-
less things. There's nothing left to do.

Night falls.

I hear perfectly the silence of the house.

12

A few hours later I get ready for my date with Alexandre.

I switch on all the lights, I check our five rooms—living room, bedroom, bedroom, kitchen, dining room. Five
rooms that resume their main function when Maria isn't
there.

When Maria isn't there the hours unfurl in a single
breath, they have no name, are not divided into chapters
like a story.

Alexandre and I.

The words come from somewhere else. Thoughts too,
my own and the stories that I'm not supposed to tell. A
dream of Maria's. The earthquake in Armenia. Survivors.
Ghosts. And another earthquake, this one in San
Francisco.

As soon as we're out on the street Alexandre puts his
arm around my waist. He kisses me. I am outside.

All words, all deeds, are movements from outside.
Alexandre doesn't realize that: he kisses me, he thinks
that I'm kissing him too, that it comes from inside.

He listens to me. This you can understand: a man and
a woman are together in a restaurant, the woman talks,
the man listens, slowly nodding his head. Now and then
she stops, she tries to figure out what she just said, they
smile at each other. Discomfort is in the air, especially
around the woman. Here, fortunately, you can talk without

interruption, there are plenty of anecdotes. Plenty of comedies, plenty of dramas are possible. The man opens another bottle of wine. The third. The woman smokes a cigarette, but it's not her, she is not this woman who is smoking. She says that she's worried about her child. The man knows very well that he's on the outside, because it's not his child. The woman is thinking about another man, the child's father, or about someone she doesn't yet know. A man who can answer when she talks about the child. All this is understandable. They are together now but the woman, in spite of all her words, is keeping everything for herself. Love does not extend this far.

Alexandre says I'm aloof. But I'm sometimes just the opposite. I plaster myself against him as if I were truly in love. A person whose life consists of being passionate, of being in love. I close my eyes, I swallow everything. The present, the empty sky, the exploding night. After that he insists on spending the night here. And of course he falls asleep before I do. All the men I've ever known have fallen asleep before I do.

The next morning he's surprised not to find me beside him. I tell him we aren't in a romantic movie. There isn't just one bedroom with a huge bed and open windows. There are two bedrooms and a woman who hides her head under her little daughter's pillow.

I don't feel well. I didn't sleep and the alcohol has swollen the little blue veins on my hands.

I want Alexandre to leave. I want to go to work, to shelve books, answer requests, be polite, even pleasant, then go home at five o'clock and wait for Maria, wait for her to come and give me an Eskimo kiss so that everything is mended.

Alexandre says there's no room for him or for anyone else in this love. There is this love, and too much solitude around it.

That's not it.

In the beginning it was true, Maria filled all the love in my heart, so completely that something was hollowed out just beneath it. You fill your heart and while you're filling it, it drains. Or the reverse, like holes you dig in the sand: they fill up with water, you dig more holes and the water keeps rising and rising. In the end, the castle is built on quicksand. Days pass, years, everything turns in the same direction, a single direction for a lifetime. A wound, a joy that is too great, it comes back and keeps coming back, forever.

With Maria, in the beginning, it was like this: I didn't stop wanting to be with her. I would beg her to go to sleep and when she finally did, I would wait for her to wake up. Worse: at night I always opened my eyes just a few seconds before she did. I'd wake up and I'd know that at any moment now I'd hear her little omnipotent voice in the dark. When I had to go back to the library I began to love my job, because it left my mind free enough to think about Maria. If a day was too busy, if I didn't have a chance that day to call up my images of Maria, I'd feel disoriented, abandoned. I was abandoned by thoughts about Maria.

In time, of course, I became accustomed to her. I mean, a more normal place, an easier place was found for everything. But my love for her will never be a reasonable love. Nor should any love. It must be everything. With someone as marvellous as Maria, that love comes close to being everything.

Before she was born, it was never enough. I would

put my hands on the skin of a man, I'd dig in and it wasn't enough or it was too much, which amounts to the same thing.

Today, something in me has become my love for Maria. A love that, at times, fills the present perfectly.

Alexandre is wrong. What he says can't be true. No love can take the place of another. No. It's something quite different.

There is the fact that I always have someone with me, because of Maria, I am always with someone, with her, with everything that's alive. I have always been, I have always felt that presence in me, I have always been aware of that force, and now it has a name too. That is what Alexandre doesn't possess. He doesn't see it.

13

In San Francisco, they've begun to search through the rubble. Cars were crushed between the two levels of a bridge. Clocks stopped at the very moment when the earthquake occurred.

They don't know what they will find. Occasionally something amazing happens. Last year, after a landslide or a mine cave-in, I don't remember which, a little two-year-old girl was found in a cave. She was singing. That was what they heard. A little voice singing under the ground, protected by a wall of rocks. Two days alone in the dark, and she was singing, she was practicing talking.

Life is incredible.

This time, under the bridge, they aren't holding out much hope. We see them working and we see more and more of the white sheets that cover bodies. The camera moves in closer, there is a man crying with his two sons.

He wants a miracle: that his third child be brought out.
He digs with his hands. There's no hope.

Last night we saw Felix outside on the balcony. We
don't know what he was doing there. He was wearing grey
pajamas with a red teddy bear on the back. Small, very
small. Barefoot. I wanted to go over and see what was
going on, then the door opened, someone pulled him by
the arm and the door closed again.

Maria says Felix is silent at daycare. He doesn't laugh,
he hardly ever talks. I don't want to see that image.

Maria didn't cry today, she is a big girl. She made a
giant sculpture out of maple leaves, popcorn, and all sorts
of other treasures. She was given permission to spend the
afternoon in the other class, with Lise; that's where she
sees Felix, he's with the younger children. He doesn't ask
for anything, but Lise often takes him in her arms.

Jeanne is here with Gabriel again. We don't want to
talk about Felix, not right away. We don't know what
we're waiting for, but we're waiting. For the time being
there are things to explain: Why is "Bibi and Geneviève"
finished? Why is tomorrow Wednesday? Why isn't Jacques
here? Is a wolf a monster? And what sound does it make
when a bridge collapses?

A little later, the children are asleep and Jeanne and I
are watching "Thirtysomething" on TV. Another story
that could be ours: one of the girls, Hope, can't work
because she's found a diary that was kept during the war by
a woman who used to live in her house. She's completely
taken up with reading it. At the same time, there is her
desire to be present, to forget nothing, to experience
everything and be aware she's doing so. During the war: a
description of the woman waiting for a husband who has

been reported missing, a dead baby, a description of the garden, of the house, of her husband who has been found. For Hope, now: the desire to have a second child, questions about that desire and about the traces that you can, that you must leave behind. Like that diary, like the rose-bushes in a garden.

And for us there is that eternal question about how to live: how to be two, three, or four, how to sleep, how to love, to stop sleeping, to look at the time or at images, to pin pictures to the wall. How to open a door, to read someone else's newspaper, how to imagine the end. How?

14

She said she wanted to come to work with me today. She pretends she's reading, she says, Look, I know how to read. That means, I know how to be quiet. She says that she's going to stay there forever, that I won't come and get her. From daycare, she means. Her little mouth starts to quiver. No, Maria, of course not, this is a Grandma day.

I had another dream about her: she was being taken away from me. There was a form in her bed, but it wasn't Maria. I could hear the black cat's little bell and then it was too late, she wasn't there any more.

That dream created so much noise: she wasn't there, she was no longer sleeping peacefully in her bed. She had gone away, it was a dream but in reality, because of the dream, she had nonetheless gone away a little. That's how fear can bore a hole in the present.

We are there, the two of us, a voice tells me that we're both there: look carefully, fill yourself with this present time. We take a cookie sheet and with two little spoons we drop dough for cookies that we'll bake and decorate in a little while. Maria, so industrious. The voice tells me to be present, even more present, to forget nothing, to imprint this image on myself forever. Hurry now, print it, because the days are passing, because there will be another day and then school, short hair, long hair, red tights that run, witch and pirate costumes, sweaters, borrowed coats that are too big, too loose, phone calls, postcards. The days pass and nothing is ever the same. Our heads ought to be a huge photo album. They aren't, and it's always too late for one thing or another.

Today, Maria counted her kisses: she says, Three thousand, a shower, a mountain of kisses. She said, I belong to Grandma a little and to you a lot. She said that. She added as she threw her arms around my neck, I love you too much. She throws back her head, mimicking someone who loves someone else too much. Then she switches to another game, she says, I'm going to make a nice American truck.

I don't know what that is. It's not like what she calls the marmelish she spreads on her hot-dog bun. And it isn't like when she says there are lots of candies on the shores of the Nile.

She draws a truck, I don't know how these things happen, but it's an American truck.

The Geography of Dreams

You may want to describe everything in detail. Or to sum-
marize it all. To hold onto only what matters. Odours.
Paper. The man who spent four days under the wrecked
bridge. His survival. That of the six hundred people now
homeless. Which brings us back to the children, alone
amid the ruins in Armenia.

Here: Maria's dream, always the same one.

I hear her struggling, saying in her faint little voice
that she doesn't want to, no, I don't want to. Her agitation
growing. Her swollen cheeks on daycare days.

Her father. The little suitcase.

Her drawings in which there are three figures, a daddy,
a child, a mummy with short hair like the child's. Their
jewellery. The sun in the right-hand corner. The moon in
the left.

Behind the window, the sky has become transparent.
No leaves now, no carpet of yellow leaves.

Alexandre and I: weeks of yes and no. Then, Alexandre
grows tired of Albanie. Or the reverse. It doesn't matter.

I am inside Maria's sadness and in that sadness everything is immense. In the morning it's insane, quick, hurry

up, quick I love you, quick, don't cry, Maria. In the end I'm the one who cries the most.

I tell Jeanne, it's a broken little life.

I also exaggerate about what has kept me away from Alexandre.

I'm not ready for anything.

It's quite obvious to Jeanne that something's wrong. That I'm preventing myself from breathing. That I keep repeating the same story.

It's a mistake to be alone. If anything were to go wrong, even something minor, if I should drop dead in the kitchen or, worse, if I should die in front of Maria, how could she ask for help, how could she live without me, and above all with the image of me dead?

Jeanne thinks my anxiety is spoiling my pleasure at being with Maria. And even: other children's despair is casting a shadow over Maria's happiness.

Open your eyes, says the voice, fill yourself with the present.

For Jeanne, all that matters now is to decorate our windows for Hallowe'en, to prepare that surprise for our children. So fate will be marked by that small miracle later on.

Unforgettable image: the four of us dressed up as Batman, four cold, giggling bats afraid of nothing, heads full of clear and savage ways to defend ourselves. A festive evening like on the night of a real storm: there's no school tomorrow.

2

The next morning, in a brief moment of weakness, I did something a little irresponsible.

When I woke up I saw Maria standing by my bed,

holding her little black cat. She wasn't moving. She was waiting for something. I got up thinking out loud, it isn't school, after all, it's not the day of her first communion. What I felt was something like anger. I called Madame Raymond and told her Maria was sick to her stomach from the candy. Same thing for daycare. Now we can spend this day together, pretending that we're sick.

We learned just now that there has been another earthquake, in Algeria this time. On television they explained how the continents shift and approach one another, and said that billions of years from now there will be no more Mediterranean. And that's why there are earthquakes.

During that report and afterwards, Maria didn't look calm for one second: she was making connections in her head. She told me about her dream, the one in which she said I don't want.

I said, Don't want what, Maria? She said, I don't want earthquakes, I don't want our house to disappear. That was when I decided that I'd have to do something about our dreams, not our night dreams but the ones we dream when we're awake, the ones in which there's a place reserved for us in a train, the ones in which Maria wants everything— cold and hot, sweet and salty, everything. I took a big notebook with a red cover and we drew a house on the first page.

It's a two-storey house and between the floors there's a staircase just for the two of us. The bedrooms are upstairs: our sleep is protected. Nothing is ever dirty and when things are no longer useful they simply go away. There are telephones everywhere and from every window we can see the leaves on a tree. Our sleep is protected.

I have always liked houses. I could be defined as a girl who likes houses, and also glaciers. One day the man I loved, the one who never left his dirty socks under the bed, asked me to define myself in one sentence. It was a kind of test. He wanted to know if he should sleep with me on the rug in his office, or if we should wait and do it comfortably, in his bed. It didn't occur to me to say, I'm someone who likes houses. I said, Shutters cast a strange kind of light on the floor. That was an image of my solitude. He liked it anyway, because we slept together on the rug in his office.

Maria's father and I always used to go and visit houses. Buying one was out of the question, of course, but on Sunday mornings we'd look at the Open House listings in the paper, we'd select one or two that were surrounded by trees, with a white kitchen and two bathrooms, and we'd go there. I always wore bright-red lipstick for the occasion. The sun turned me into a smiling young woman, never lonely, never sad, never separated. Maria would come with us: that made us even more charming. It was sheer happiness. Visiting houses gave us an idea of what happiness was, of what it could be.

This is why I enjoy spending Hallowe'en with Maria so much: because I can look inside all the houses. Beacons call to us from the front doors: you can transform the fate of at least thirty persons in a single evening.

In one house, for instance, we see wallpaper on the walls, flowers everywhere, and a lot of gilt-framed photographs. Weddings, births. The woman who opens the door has forgotten to take off her apron, she bends down to pick up a note from her husband, "I won't be coming home tonight," she blinks just a little, we close the door, the candies have been chosen with care and wrapped in a little black bag.

I don't know what others might have thought when they knocked at our door. Even Jeanne was horrified, because we weren't ready. The news was on, there were some children waiting at the door, and we weren't ready. And then there was Jeanne's urge to cry, which she'd been holding back since morning because she had seen Jacques with another girl.

I've never understood Jeanne's jealousy. It's a jealousy after the fact and devoid of love, as if no man could ever love again after he'd known her.

As for me, jealousy means that somewhere, some day, another woman will be able to touch Maria's cheek. She'll tell her stories, wash her hair, put her in a new dress for a party. It's only at such times that I consider stopping someone else's life.

Now Maria wants me to draw a map of the world. She makes two Xs to show me exactly where we are. She means that there's a place in the universe where we happen to be. She wants to be quite certain about that. She thinks of what I've told her about the shifting continents, she sees them as rafts and she sees us, with our souls, on one of the rafts.

After that, she says she has a surprise for me. She tells me to wait, and when she comes back she has an old picture of my first communion: blue bolero, blue pleated skirt, stockings that are too beige, too heavy, a white mantilla, a priest, an unknown godmother. A smile that looks too much like a smile.

That's not a dream, Maria.

She says nothing.

While I, I see all those times, unphotographed, when I didn't go to school, when I didn't do what I was supposed to do. The same sense of guilt—slight, very slight—next to the same sense of victory: we have earned a day.

3

It wasn't a good idea, of course. I mean playing hooky, the two of us in our pajamas with a red notebook on our laps. Now I must explain to Maria that some days are special events and others aren't. That's the kind of thing Maria can't understand. For her, every day is glorious.

I tell her, Tonight we're going to make a sky. We'll imagine everything the sky says, the number of times it changes in a day, a week, a year. At the end of this year we'll draw an airplane and that will be our travel dream.

Maria selects a place on the map: the Arctic Circle. In her atlas you can see an igloo and a big polar bear. In mine there are names I circled long ago: Alaska, Inuvik, Baffin Island. Maria chooses this place to make me happy, she knows how much I like glaciers and bays and fjords and the Valley of Ten Thousand Smokes!

I give her my word that we will take that trip, and we leave the house as if it were an ordinary morning, each of us with a photo of glaciers in her pocket: they help us to get through the day.

That evening, Maria asked me to draw the sky I'd promised her. She never forgets anything.

We hesitate between a daytime and a nighttime sky, but the daytime sky wins out. Blue, with clouds descending towards us. Both of us think of her father, we don't know if we should draw his silhouette in the airplane. I say yes.

Later, I have another dream.

We are in a desert of ice, we have to tell a woman that she has given birth to a little girl with no arms.

We tell her.

She smiles. The little girl is so pretty, all bundled up in fur.

4

Maria's grief has not been healed. Lise thinks that there's too much noise, too many children here, and that her head is filled with enough things as it is. Maria is sometimes angry too, sometimes she's rather like Felix, with a little look of submission. The worst look for a child to have.

Lise invents nothing, she simply says that Maria is lucky to have a grandmother like hers and that we should take advantage of her. She doesn't says the words "to face up to life as it is." For her there is no modern theory to help you shed your guilt. Only life, sad or joyous, that unfurls before her eyes.

Now and then, not too often, we play hooky again. We don mitts and tuques and walk along the street. There we find all the things we like. First, the red-white-and-blue barber's pole. We adore it, just as we adore everything that turns. Then, the fronts of houses. Red brick, with open gates. In store windows, ribbons, faucets, coffee pots ... And things that turn: mobiles, tops, planets. Further along, we go into a store and study all the Babar toys, one by one. I tell Maria that we like Babar better than Batman, but she hasn't decided yet. For her it's a matter of knowing in which clan we place ourselves, knowing what we find beautiful, what we find ugly, knowing what period we like. Finally it's yes, and Maria leaves the store with a little Babar brooch pinned to her coat. That evening we leaf through a fashion magazine and

Maria picks out a dress for me, one with sequins, and we glue it onto the third page of our dream book.

Occasionally we meet someone on the street. Once it was Alexandre, and Maria asked, What's your name? He gave us a faint smile. My aloofness surprised him. I don't feel anything. Not a thing.

Jeanne took a Polaroid photo of me. She thinks I'm being hard on Alexandre, but that my behaviour makes me photogenic.

Say something, she told me, and don't look too natural.

I said, This is my dream, to be detached, to be a silhouette that stands out against a cold blue sky.

Jeanne is convinced that deep inside me there is a door I've left ajar for Maria's father. I just have to close it completely and begin again with someone else.

I don't know how to do that. I've never begun my life over. I've never looked for someone who could be my love.

In the photo I look very much like a woman who has committed a murder. Maria says, That's Albanie. We pin her to the wall, next to the photo of Maria's father.

It will soon be Christmas. We're getting ourselves into a frenzy around that theme. First, the Three Wise Men follow the star sent by the Eskimo. Next comes the natural order of things: birth, death, and two lists of presents. It will be Maria's first double Christmas.

Sometimes I'm a little scatterbrained and I sit on the kitchen floor. I'm someone who wipes her hands on her sweater in the afternoon. I take pauses, I think very hard about the midnight sun. Maria shows me the white lines in the sky, like a kind of cloud. She transforms surfaces, she claps her hands. She says, Mummy's sick, and she strokes my brow, so precisely. We are not alone. We often tremble because of some unknown thing the earth does, or the continents, and we are not alone. Objects spin and fly for us. With them and with our hearts, we build memory.

5

Tears are always waiting in our bodies, they accumulate, they form little scraps of universe in our soul, exactly like the dreams in our dream book, and then one day, at the first opportunity, they escape.

This morning I started to cry while I was reading the newspaper. Floods of tears. All the tears that had accumulated since Maria's father left.

At first there was the kind of joy that we've been seeing and hearing everywhere for the past few days. It's because of the passages through the Berlin Wall. Something incredible is happening again, people climbing onto the Wall, others going through the passage, they hold out their hands, they're going to the West, to buy some object they have dreamed about, to touch a person they haven't seen for so long, then they come back, night falls, and now the silence has gone.

After that, it's in the paper, there's another child who needs a home. No suitable parents have been found, no one knows who could cope with so much solitude.

I looked at Maria sitting on the floor with her imaginary characters and I couldn't understand, couldn't make the connection between her laughter and the other child's despair. Between my past and present lives.

I have always thought that all things are interconnected, even if it's sometimes by an invisible thread, and that we must pay close attention, because if we lose just one small thing we could drop all the rest. I was thinking that a badly buttoned shirt was linked to the disorder of the universe.

And so when I found myself alone again with Maria, it all began with a dry little sound in the house. Then the landlord came to tell us there was a problem with the furnace. They fixed it, but for days our feet were freezing. And finally her father gave me a vague look and told me, I'm moving out. As if he were saying, I'm going to change my shirt. Or rather, as though he weren't saying, you have to change your face, to become another person, a woman who talks on the radio for instance, in a low voice, a woman who knows how to remain mysterious, but that's not what happens and I can't love you any more the way you are. He meant, like this, with my cold feet and my fear that things around me would disappear. He didn't want to say you and Maria, but it was me and Maria. The only order in the universe that I'm aware of.

And today, these tears because I don't know how to restore order to the universe. I don't know how to be that joy on the other side of the Wall, or that sorrow, I don't know how to find myself again inside Maria's smile.

When night fell, she poured all her marbles into one of my shoes, and when I went to put them on I saw them: they could have been planets against a black background.

At that moment, I saw myself entering into Maria's smile. Her presence is constantly directed at me and that's how she can always settle everything.

6

Mummy, look! Maria points to the window and we get a glimpse of Felix across the street. He's all alone. He's kicking the fence. His shoes are too big.

We watch him for a while, then Maria asks me if he's waiting for his mummy.

Maybe he is, Maria.

We decide to go over and ask him.

It's cold out. Maria doesn't want to wear mittens, she shoves her hands in her pockets to look grown-up. She says, This is like an investigation by Inspector Gadget.

We wait a good five minutes because there's a dog on the other side of the street. We don't like dogs.

Felix looks at us, he recognizes Maria, then he starts kicking the fence again.

Are you waiting for your mummy? Maria asks him.

He doesn't answer. This really is like an investigation by Inspector Gadget.

Then Maria starts to play with him. They make marks in the mud. With a piece of branch they draw a square, a rectangle, a triangle.

I ask him where his parents are. He points to the house.

Time to go home, Maria.

We wave goodbye.

Later, because for her too all things are connected, Maria draws her little sister in our notebook. Her name is Salome.

Just now Salome is asleep, but Maria swears that she'll do lots of things on the other pages. You'll see, she'll come to the Arctic Circle with us.

Then Maria wants to know if I'm old. I say, I'm a very very young mummy. She says she's afraid I'll get dead.

I can't stop thinking about Felix. I can see him very easily in the "Can you give this child a home?" column. We could read his story: his mother leaves him in the park and tells him to wait there for his father. Her voice is impossibly sweet. She leaves the house, decides which way to go. She walks into the subway, a train is just emerging from the tunnel, she throws herself in front of it. Ever since then he has been alone. He is looking for another mummy.

But it's not that.

Jeanne says that she saw his parents once and that we mustn't get carried away.

Maria asks again if I'm going to get dead. I say no. But if I do I'll wink at her from the sky. I won't get dead, but if it ever does happen you'll still have Jeanne and Gabriel, and Daddy and Grandma and Grandpa and Salome, and there will also be Christmas and Easter and Epiphany and strange little winking lights in the sky.

7

Salome is beginning to have her own story. Like Felix she wears shoes that are too big for her, she drinks 7-Up with a straw, she is two years old, she has curly black hair and we've adopted her. One day Salome went out and met a ghost who had two little black eyes, and then at the end of the road she saw an amazing number of fish.

Is that where we found her, Maria?

Yes. In the sea with the fish.

For several days now we've been observing Felix through the window. On the day of the first snowfall he tried to collect snowflakes in a saucepan. Another time, he wanted to tame a stray cat. Maria went out to ask the cat, What's your name? and Felix said, Snowflake, his name is Snowflake.

Maria said, It's Felix's cat. He's trying to make him drink 7-Up with a straw.

I still haven't seen his mother, but his father is always sitting at the window like a ghost in a rocking chair. A real ghost.

I've given in. Maria will come to the library with me today. She'll be a good girl and stay in the children's section. At noon we'll eat our lunch together and she'll tell me everything that has happened to her friends, she'll say, Life is appalling, she heard someone say that on television.

Madame Raymond gestures towards the woman who is here again, sitting at a table in the back of the room. She's been coming here for months. We know nothing about her except that there was a fire in her apartment and the smell of it stayed on her clothes for a long time. All she said was that the smell was like danger, always there, always present.

We read her name on her card, it's Agnes.

That name doesn't suit her.

Could she be writing a book about the fire?

Back at the house, Maria adds a new adventure for Salome: the adventure of a library.

Salome discovers a dictionary with the names of every kind of medicine. Now she can take care of everyone she loves. Even Felix. Even his cat.

8

The wind is howling into the dryer vent. It's like a private drama.

There are piles of laundry all over the house. Some are too high and they lean like the Tower of Pisa.

Mismatched socks are lined up on my bed. There's a smell of food that seems to be waiting for something. Jeanne and I know what it all represents—the piles of laundry, the wind, the food.

It snowed again and Maria played outside for most of the afternoon. In the past she wouldn't get excited, she'd hold her head up, a little snobbish, she used to say she didn't like the snow. Now that she's older she adores snow, she has become a real child. It will please her father. Fathers always want their children to be real children. They don't like them to close their eyes when they listen to a song, or to cry because the song is sad; they think that life is a safari and that the snow, the circus, skating rinks are natural places for children.

Maria shouts at me to come and see the little girls on television. She is fascinated. I don't know if it's because of the parallel bars or the costumes or the movements of the little gymnasts. Undoubtedly she's seen something I haven't noticed.

I ask if she'd like to do what they are doing. She spins around, her arms are all excited, she says, Yes, I could be like them and you'll hide in a little door to watch me do my exercises.

There we are. A tiny space inside Maria has become clear and bright. What fascinates her is that I could be present, hidden behind a glass door, and she wouldn't know, and she'd do everything she could to continue being loved.

Life is not a safari, it is the dream of such a love. The

only thing we truly desire is for someone to be with us, for that someone to hide behind a door and watch us, to hold our hand when we go to the dentist or to the most decisive meeting of our life.

Perhaps that is why Felix and Agnes are now part of all of my days. Perhaps I am becoming that hidden person who watches as they live. I see their motions as in a silent film. Sometimes I add titles with their words. Most of the time, though, there's no mystery. They are there, they open their eyes, they close them, tears run down their cheeks. They are an example of what is sick about life. They are the life that turns like the dragon's eyes in Maria's book.

9

We've put up our Christmas tree. The lights, Maria's big smile. She wanted a star at the top of the tree. That's a lot prettier than an angel, she said.

Some days I am really a character, not in Maria's life but in a movie. That night I saw myself from the back, a woman trimming her Christmas tree. Everything has been chosen so carefully, every star, every ornament, like a question that's very important for her. The woman is dressed in grey, a colour she likes. Her clothes are soft and loose. Aloud, she says that she always looks as if she's wearing pajamas. Three times she checks to be sure the front door is locked. Sometimes she's a woman without a child. This evening for instance she's sitting by the telephone, crying over something that she's lost or that she's never had.

Maria always looks forward to when it gets dark, so we can turn on the lights. Days pass waiting for this small miracle.

There has been no sign of Felix for two weeks now. Snowflake often goes past his door, but we don't see Felix's footprints in the snow. There's no Christmas tree in his living room. Just a plastic Santa Claus nailed to the brick.

Agnes has come to the library every afternoon. She continues to write on loose sheets of paper. Sometimes when I walk past her I see triangles drawn in the margin. Yesterday she gave us a Chinese Christmas card. She signed it, Agnes. She speaks with an accent.

Christmas is a group of days cut from a magazine. Every day is a collage with many colours, two housecoats, a TV set that's turned on for no reason, animal-shaped cookies that we eat in the morning, and everything in the house that makes noise.

Suddenly a voice says, Mummy; you turn around, your heart beating a little faster than usual, you see an amazing smile and the little girl who is there. All she wants is just one moment—and this too is cut out of the magazine— when you hold her in your arms.

It's like saying thank you.

Thank you for being there.

Then, as quickly as she arrived, the little girl goes off to play in the part of the house that's her favourite today. All of that only lasted a few seconds, but in our memories it's a central square with long avenues leading off in every direction.

In the photo Maria is sitting in front of the tree; she seems to be saying, see what we've done, there are no pets, no miniature reproductions of microwave ovens, no mini-cradle with a fake mini-sister asleep in it, there's only me and the tree with its lights.

Her father hasn't come. So there will be another set

of snapshots, images that can never be part of our memories, which will turn up unexpectedly one day and pro-
voke a brief short-circuit between the two hemispheres of
my brain.

As for us, my parents and me, we seem to be uncon-
cerned. Things don't happen twice, even though, as I've
already said, they continue to happen. There are never
two phone calls to announce that a family member has
died, decapitated on the road. Even if the doorbell keeps
ringing. What happens elsewhere will continue to happen there. Even Felix: we haven't thought about him all
that much.

In the last picture, very fuzzy because Gabriel took it,
you can see Jeanne and me, a little too far to the left, not
looking at the camera because we were dancing and we
were hungover. You can't see that there are only two children looking at us. A little more and we could be sitting
on a table, legs pulled up, arms hugging our knees, each of
us beside her lover's bed, as beautiful as Liza Minnelli in
her latest video.

Jeanne has written on the back of the picture: Albanie
and me, as pretty as anybody else if not prettier, Christmas
1989. Still, we both have that smile that belongs to no
one but us because we knew that there were only two children to look at us. Everything was included in that look.

10

Maria told her father, If you go away Mummy will cry. I
wish I could stick my head inside a kitchen cupboard. I
wish I had two heads, one for myself and one for others.
And I wish I didn't type words backwards.

I'm writing a letter to Maria's father. Typing, so that he'll understand. That I'm not crying. That Maria has invented a little sister she calls Salome, and now Salome is the one who stays hidden in her corner at the daycare. That he can tell her stories about Salome. That he could even come to a movie with us, or for lunch, or anything else as long as Maria agrees.

Yesterday Gabriel, still in his Batman costume, put his arms around Maria and whispered a secret in her ear. I think it had to do with his father. I don't know. They didn't laugh. Maria was suddenly much smaller than he. He looked as if he wanted to encompass everything. He was her big brother, her cousin, someone like that. Afterwards they played for a long time with Gabriel's toy computer. All we could hear was a man's voice saying: "Press the red button" and "Well done" and then, "Fantastic!" Later on we saw their two little faces appear in the doorway. They came closer, they shouted simultaneously to each of us, Stay here, stay here!

Now it's Jeanne's turn to be worried. For me it's a normal state of affairs, but for her ... Her long black hair no longer seems to be following her. She's afraid of being too strong, afraid that one day all her grief will sneak up on her from behind.

We're drinking wine. We're in a café where nothing seems to be meant for us.

It's the same uneasy feeling. Again, that sense of being in the wrong place. An urge to go home, to sit in the living room and gather up the scattered pieces of Maria's jigsaw puzzle.

Jeanne thinks she'll never again catch a glimpse of a nice, attractive man coming towards her. A total stranger, someone new who tastes fresh and doesn't say, I'll call you next week.

We're between Christmas and New Year's. Everyone seems to be part of a family. We can't take it any more.

On the television, which sits on the counter next to a big bouquet of white flowers, we can see again some images of recent events in Germany and Czechoslovakia. A crowd gathers and resolves to say no. Calmly. And then in Romania, not so calmly. We don't know what could happen here, but the urge to say no must spread this far, to us.

People walk along the street smiling. In their smiles you can see pain—slight, a mere thread, but a pain that is ancient. Others do everything possible to get into or out of their cars. They run their hands through their hair. Sometimes they make the same motion for someone else. They are happy or sad. They read newspapers, they declare bankruptcy. They look at the time and wish they could spend the day sleeping.

Now the television is showing another famine in Ethiopia. Of course they show us the worst: a woman holds out her child to the camera. The child is crying without tears, flies stuck to his lips, his eyelids. There is nothing we can say about something that would drive Jeanne and me out of our minds. We can't go on. We look away.

At another table, a very young couple never stops kissing. The boy has long hair, it's back in style, and just looking at him I find myself back in the corridor at school, where love has been given to me because a boy with long hair is pressing me into a locker, holding me in his arms. I was sixteen and I thought I was loved. Life was so powerful that it pressed me against a locker. But desire changed, and each time I discovered a new form, a new body for that desire.

And now Jeanne and Albanie are looking away again, inside them the murder of the world is as powerful as life. As peaceful. Like a trolley running along an underground passage. They take money from their purses to pay. Slightly drunk, they think they've lost their keys again. They open the door, the air makes them even heavier and at the same time more determined. They want to catch all the words that are whispered behind them. They glide, they don't drop the chocolate Christmas trees they're holding. They arrive at Albanie's house, Maria and Gabriel are at the window with the new baby-sitter. Across the street Felix is there, he's playing in the snow, even more alone than usual.

11

Felix rips the plastic Santa Claus off the brick and buries it in the snow. He pounds on the door, no one opens it. He digs up Santa Claus and starts to talk to him. Ten minutes later he knocks again, the door opens, he throws Santa back in the snow and goes into the house.

The new baby-sitter is called Nathalie. A real sitter's name. Gabriel and Maria like her. They listen to Pagliaro's record with her and when we arrive they shout at us *sans ton coeur je suis seul sur terre*. They have been dancing and they're all red.

They have ideas about everything. Gabriel asks Jeanne if she has ever met anyone *seul sur terre* on the street. He means another Jacques. He takes paper and pencil and draws a little tent on the globe. That's his image of being alone on the earth.

Maria has drawn Felix inside the tent. She says, It used to be Salome. But we adopted her. And now we have to adopt Felix because he's always alone in the snow outside his house.

Several days off work.

We use the time to put away the clothes that are too small for Maria. A white summer dress with little pink-and-blue designs breaks my heart. She had just started to walk. In that dress she was even more unreal, I mean her beauty was unreal, it was too much. I didn't dare believe it. On her first birthday the grandparents were there, and my sisters and all our friends. We were all connected by her, by the way we all looked at her. You can see it quite clearly in the pictures. And even without pictures I remember everything, the solitary candle that she didn't want to blow out, her surprise and then her fear when we all sang together. I also remember a Christmas when I was so sorry not to be alone with her and her father. There was too much agitation and I couldn't really absorb the moment for my future memory. I couldn't capture all her smiles, all her gestures. I kept thinking about the life that was escaping me and I could do nothing about it. It still goes on. Emotions emerge from us, they swell up like events and then they die. There's nothing we can do about it.

Maria keeps asking me to tell her about when she was a baby. What she did, what she ate. And most of all, who was with her. Daddy?

In the end every garment possesses a history. Every dress, every pair of pajamas is associated with a first time. We fill boxes with the brilliant fragments of the time we've had so far. We are the centre of the universe. Each house is the centre of the universe and we can depict the world this way: as a globe with countless little tents on it drawn by a child. What goes on inside the tent is a unique story that starts afresh a thousand times.

12

Maria took one of her baby pictures from my album and pasted it into our dream book. I realized it this morning. It's a black-and-white photo, a very tight close-up of her face and on the back is written, Maria, two months.

On the other page she drew a Christmas tree covered with ornaments of every colour. She came up behind me, she put her head against my neck and asked, Next Christmas will I still be little? I said yes, you'll still be a little girl, but she didn't believe me. She said she'd be glad when she turned four this summer, but just a little glad, not completely.

She is beginning to understand what time is: a car that drives past and doesn't give you a chance.

Tomorrow we go back to work. Maria knows. That's why she put her picture and the one of the Christmas tree next to each other in our dream book. From now on, for her and for me, those two images will be linked forever.

The day before yesterday, New Year's Eve, Maria slept at her father's and Jeanne and I went to a party. Came home late, both fairly drunk.

The evening progressed as these things usually do. At first you have good conversations with people you don't know all that well. You keep looking around. You can't concentrate. Then suddenly the music gets us very worked up. A piece that we like, that we've liked in the past. We become even younger, we stop pretending to talk. We dance. We drink. When the time comes to wish each other Happy New Year, we slip away a little, we'd like to keep our emotions inside.

One thing happened. Jacques came into the apartment around one a.m., Jeanne threw her arms around him and he pushed her away. Then she was the person crying in the kitchen. There's always one, and this time it was Jeanne. She wanted them to be able to say hello, hi, but men who are aloof like Jacques forget everything and in their oblivion they take away something of us as well. A little kernel of passion. Afterwards, one can no longer begin again.

I took a bottle of bubbly and went to join her in the kitchen. She said she was crying over something else, because she'd been wrong about life, which is a series of ruptures that are accomplished more or less successfully. Most of all, she was crying because someone had pushed her away, and he'd done so during the first hour of the new year. I know Jeanne. It wouldn't have mattered who did it, but not that particular deed, above all not that.

We kept on drinking, then we started dancing again because it was our favourite song. The lyrics repeated *a lifetime, one whole lifetime* in Italian. The music was *a whole lifetime*.

I wanted it to last a thousand years, but nothing lasts a thousand years except the sea, rocks, landscapes. And no one has managed yet to be a landscape.

But I was the music.

I danced till four a.m. without exactly realizing that there were other people. Jeanne too, I think. At four, someone took her in his arms, lifted her gently and put her to bed. As for me, I don't like sleeping anywhere but in my own bed, so I took a taxi home. Plenty of details could have captured my attention, but they didn't. When I got home I looked at myself in the mirror to see what the others had seen, but there was nothing. Just a tired face on the verge of disappearing. So I went to my room and collapsed into bed.

The next day I called Maria to wish her Happy New Year and then something else happened. Her father asked me to come over. I wasn't sure what to do. I said yes.

He opened the door.

I immediately took Maria in my arms.

His family was already there and they wished me all the things you're supposed to. I was thinking very seriously about the aspirins in my purse.

Finally he said, I'll bring her back to you tomorrow, and for once I was the one who walked out the door, leaving Maria with her father and his whole family. It was the worst thing that could happen to me.

It was this morning that she made the remark about next Christmas, and tonight she added another: But I love you.

Meaning, if I love you why should I grow up and be more and more apart from you?

13

This is my dream.

We are visiting a house that resembles the one in our book. The little girl likes everything, she roots around in the cupboards, she rolls on the floor, she opens the bird-cage while the owners are trying to explain things to me. A man in a jacket shows me the plans. It's Alexandre. The man and woman are at a loss because he keeps stroking the nape of my neck. Then the little girl shuts herself into one of the bedrooms upstairs and we can't get to her. The door is locked and, as in the dream of a dream, I can't climb the stairs.

Then the three of us are in a park. I put my hand in front of my mouth because something has started to quiver. In my palm are all my teeth, which have fallen out.

I wake with a start because Maria is standing beside my bed, crying. Her grief is vast and silent and she can't talk about it. She says, I'm stuck, says it over and over a thousand times. It's a nightmare, Maria. Then she comes up to the surface and this time she starts to cry because she wants to stay here, she doesn't want to go there.

Later on I leave her in tears anyway, in the arms of a teacher whom I too am starting to hate. But I go to work nonetheless.

As soon as I walk into the library I spot Agnes at the back of the room, like a shadow. I would like to throw myself at her, shake her, beg her to help me, but I don't do anything.

At ten o'clock Lise calls to tell me not to worry.

What's she doing?

She's making a tower out of Plasticine.

Agnes often looks at me. She has sensed that I was going to ask her something. She's going to approach me, she's going to tell me what to do for Maria, and how we can co-exist with our dreams.

She stays in her seat.

She has picked up a big book about transatlantic ships and now she's turning the pages one by one, slowly, as if she were performing a ceremony. She spends longer with some pages, stroking the pictures there.

She resembles me. She likes these stories about ships with several decks, with several berths where you can sit to write a letter or to put your jewellery back in its case. She likes what happens at night, she likes glaciers and the sea that can wash everything away.

Lunch-hour.

I leaf through a magazine where I find this story. Two sets of twins are born in a hospital somewhere in France. Their family names are almost the same. The twins are mixed up. For two years, to everyone including their own mothers, they are false twins, and then one day at the market each one finds herself looking at a little girl who is identical to herself. At first the mothers can't get over it. Each woman has two daughters: one who is hers and one who is another woman's. Neither knows which one is really hers. They decide not to change anything and now they all live together.

What is most incredible about this story is that it's true. That all of this really happened and that it too is part of life on this earth, in a city, in a house. While such things were happening, we were rocking a child or cooking or dreaming about a tooth falling out and one day, without our ever knowing why, we in turn become the focus of an unbelievable story.

I tear the pages from the magazine to show Jeanne. There are a lot of pictures.

When I go back to the books, Agnes is no longer there.

She has left a crumpled piece of paper on the table on which is written, "Dear David."

When the sky starts to change colour, I tell myself it's time to go home.

As for Maria, she goes and sits beside her boots in the cloakroom. She has seen the sky, she knows that she can wait for me and she won't have to wait too much longer.

14

The first week of the year is nearly over.

This afternoon I went back to work right after lunch. I was so pale that Madame Raymond sent me home.

In the mailbox was the Christmas card that Maria had insisted on sending me. There are two little reindeer on it, us most likely, and inside she has pretended to write a long love letter. Tonight she will ask me to read it to her while she stamps her feet impatiently, Read me what I wrote, Mummy.

I went to my bedroom and stood at the window for quite a while. For once the sun was shining brightly.

Snow.

The footprints of a man who comes home with bags of groceries. He stops, chats with his neighbour, talks about the year just ended and the one that's just now beginning. He gestures broadly. Like all of us.

Suddenly, a group of children appears. Accompanied by two adults, they are walking, each one holding onto a rope so they won't get lost. A little girl breaks away from the group, she goes up to one of the adults, then turns and heads towards the other. Like that, two or three times. She is dressed all in yellow and mauve and you can see the blond hair sticking out of her tuque. She's very excited: she talks a lot as she points to the house. It's Maria.

What's really odd is that I didn't realize it right away. It was as if she couldn't be my daughter, that little stranger outside the house and, especially, outside of me.

I was happy and at the same time utterly disconcerted. I hid so she wouldn't see me, and what was even more bizarre, I had to hide, my gaze had briefly broken into a space and a time that belonged only to Maria. I'm certain that I felt the same thing just then, the same solitude, as she did on the day she understood that she wasn't me and I wasn't her. Now I'm a grown-up, she's not me, each of us is someone else, another person.

When I told her later that I'd noticed her through the window, her reaction was the opposite of mine. Knowing that I'd seen her today when she wasn't with me meant that I was still part of her a little, even from a distance, that I will always be part of these days.

It was reassuring.

It brought her closer to the image of the little gymnasts whose mothers were watching, unbeknownst to them. Mothers are always there to some extent, that's what it said to her.

For me, she had grown too much all at once.

She wants us to write the names of all the objects around us in our dream book. She says them and I write them down. There are curtains, tables, chairs. There are records, books, shoes. And angels, the bookcase, the spoon, and the bowl full of salty little fish.

We write a lot on two pages and Maria wants to add another page with the names of the people we know. Jeanne, with her long black hair that we always want to touch. Gabriel, whose hair is blond like Maria's, and like hers as well, his little teeth that show when he smiles. And all the others with the clothes they wear, the jewellery, their toys, the way they say hello when they arrive.

Maria is fully occupied by this task. Every time she comes up with a name, she goes to the very heart of her desires. And then each thing, each object, has the power to make her existence even more real.

I too have always considered objects to be alive. All of them. Even food. When I was a little girl like Maria, I would line up my sections of orange and eat them one by one, telling those that were left not to worry, it would soon be their turn to be eaten. It suited me to think that the orange wanted to be eaten. And I reassured each section: none of them would be left on the table, alone of its kind.

Now all those things have at least two existences: one in our life and one in our dream book. They have joined the house, the sky with the airplane and three people looking out the windows, the trip to the Arctic Circle, Salome, the Christmas tree, and just beside it, the two-month-old baby named Maria. If I recapitulate properly, if I'm able to cause one image to touch another, it could result in a wonderful story for Maria. She would create all the illustrations and it would be the most beautiful book we'd ever read. It would be at our bedside like a night-light, reminding us that we exist and that we must be stronger than our fear.

To Witness

The dream in which I visit a house has recurred several times in the past few weeks. Sometimes Maria is there in the upstairs bedroom, sometimes Felix is lying across the bed, and sometimes it's Jeanne, asleep there with Gabriel.

The man who shows me around the house is also inter-changeable. Alexandre or Maria's father or some total stranger.

Once, the stranger puts his hand on my thigh, it's heavy, the hand goes inside my skin and we fall to the floor. I like that image, me on the floor with someone, in a church or an office, or here in my kitchen.

For Jeanne and me the month of February is huddled in our hearts. We think of leaving our bodies for the body of someone else, and it's at times like these that we do the worst things. For instance, we spend the evening watching a dating show on TV. We notice that every-thing takes place in the shadows while a neutral voice reads a text that is supposed to render the person clear and luminous. Without exception, each woman, each man, is shown in profile. The text refers to such modern things as communication, tennis, or Club Med vacations, but the body is a hieroglyph in an Egyptian tomb.

We continue to work, to protect our boots with wax, and to learn new songs for our children. We scribble lists that we fasten to the refrigerator door with little magnets. Telephones for me, pears and eggplants for Jeanne.

Occasionally we'll have an evening out, always at the same restaurant in case someone comes over to our table to say, It's you I've been waiting for. Inevitably we end up talking about Gabriel and Maria, and if anyone does look our way we don't even see him.

One night Jeanne meets Jacques, they go to her place and make love, mixed with a little hate. The next morning they make the bed and can't think of anything else to say. Jeanne tells me everything. She says she felt as if she was in some tale of passion with bread and knives on the table, and we burst out laughing. It's when the two of us are together that we do it best—laughing I mean—and standing off to one side of events.

At the library I haven't found any more notes written by Agnes. Perhaps David is her lover, a sailor lost at sea, who knows what. I do know that she's cold, she keeps her scarf wrapped around her neck, and when she's thinking she crosses her arms and sticks her hands in her sleeves.

Even though it's so hot in here. Occasionally when I bend down to put away a book, I have to stop because everything starts to spin. I open a book by Joyce Carol Oates and read the first sentence, which I put on the refrigerator door that night, next to a recipe for a Valentine's Day cake. The sentence can mean anything since it's like a great white desert stretching out before me: *One warm evening in August 1937 a girl in love stood before a mirror.*

We've run out of our citrus cream. We decide not to buy another jar till spring. Just now, it's too much like winter and our hands smell sometimes of wet wool, sometimes of Vicks, and sometimes of baby powder.

2

The spiders are still there. They're on the lookout for me, they like me, but I'm not happy to see them. If I do notice one I close my eyes, and they take advantage of that and multiply on the wall. Especially on those evenings when I'm a woman who's afraid of someone coming into the house to harm her. I don't say to kill her, but I am thinking "to kill her."

When I was six years old I would hear mice running inside the walls of our house. At that time there was a lot of talk about extra-terrestrials and I was afraid they'd come looking for me and put little marks on my body. Some time later, I began to fear Jesus. I'd keep my eyes open, I had to, I had to be always on guard and to summon up as many images as I could so that he wouldn't whisper in my ear that I had a vocation. Or that he'd come looking for me too.

I believed the images would leave no room for his voice. I thought of a beach-ball rolling along the ocean shore. I was a headstrong little girl in a blue bathing suit with red cherries. I laughed hard, I donned my water-wings, and I threw myself into the ocean. That was my childhood, my favourite image to counter Jesus, and I didn't want anyone to take it away.

Now it's to ward off death that I force myself to think of something cheerful. I see Maria catching the ball, I see her making friends on the beach, she shouts to me from a distance, she cups her hands around her mouth, she's a captain shouting at me to watch out for the sharks that lurk around here.

A little closer in time, she opens a chocolate heart, inside it there is pink and yellow straw, she pushes it aside and discovers all the baby chocolate hearts. She looks at me and that's it, now we really are a fantastic force. No one can see us as we sit with our feet on the table, singing a Rolling Stones song at the top of our lungs, but we are there, present, and that makes us a fantastic force.

Maria makes up another story for Salome. Two little girls are doing arts and crafts. They go to school and when they arrive there, they forget their address. They lose their mittens and they tell their mummies what they've done that day.

On television, a child puts up her hand to talk. She is given permission, she says, When someone spanks me I feel all little inside.

I turn around to see if Maria has understood. She hasn't heard anything, she is absorbed by her book, she's helping Salome count snowflakes. And then stars. And finally, things that are easier to count. She goes to look for the box of cookies. She says, Cookies are easier than stars.

I'm thinking about Felix again. There's nothing visible about him. No marks left by extra-terrestrials. No hand clouting him on the head. Nothing. But there are so many ways to become little inside. I know. I know ways for him, and for Agnes. And even for Jeanne, and for me. For the future as well. For that man who's sitting on his steps. He doesn't dare go inside. He doesn't dare look at what's happening on his planet. That's one of the things I know.

3

We showed Jeanne our dream book and it gave her an idea. For the past few days she's been going around with a video camera shooting everything she sees. It's fashionable, and it's Jeanne: she makes doubles of us, she multiplies us by ten, and in that way our life becomes a step taken beyond the images. We go past that step, past the multiples of ourselves, and what is real to us now is a landscape broken up into small pictures. We can enter it or not, we can put our memories there or, conversely, we can see there certain individuals who are present, always present. What is important is that they are there, that the mere fact of their existence creates a sense of distance.

So we're going to shoot a memory scrapbook, exactly as our parents used to do with sixteen-millimetre film. They would choose a day—a party or a holiday in New England—and we'd find ourselves outside of time, for a moment we were outside the range of our lives.

It's something I've always wanted to do: to show Maria what's gravitating around us, the stories she tells, the music, newspapers, everything.

When Maria was born, there was a little space to fill in on the second page of her Baby's Book entitled "The Event that Marked the World Today." It was just under "Today's Weather." I had written, Clouds everywhere, white clouds. The day after she was born the sun shone and the warm weather had come to stay. As for the event, I could think of nothing to write except, Maria's Birth. That was when I first got the idea of writing her a letter, for later. A very long letter that I'd write over the next twenty years.

I wanted the letter to contain notes on all the things that have the power to define us. For instance, there would be a description of the little white shirt she was wearing when we left the hospital. Her little hands moving across her face that I'd recognized right away. At night her father would rock her, he would lay her down on top of him. All the things happening to us were incredibly new. But at the same time, since we could not do otherwise, we were becoming increasingly and completely our true selves.

I often picture myself writing that letter. It happens like this: Albanie is quiet, she's sitting at a table writing a letter to Maria, for later. Her hair is still short, her glasses are on the table, and she writes: We were born on almost the same day, in the summer, twenty-seven years apart, and even now it is sometimes hard for me to acknowledge that we are not the same person.

She stands up, takes off her jeans which are too tight, gets a glass of water, and goes on: Everyone loves your name, Maria. They say that it's open and clear, exactly as I hoped, and they add that you inhabit your name perfectly, you make it even clearer, even more open. Your father hasn't been with me for a year now. I think that I loved him and he loved me too, but with you we have become so much our true selves, I mean we couldn't find enough places to put all our love. I am sure now that someone is waiting for me, a man with black hair, that he will smile at me with sad, knowing eyes, that he'll take me to a bedroom where there are grass-lined roads and it won't be my road, the one I'm alone on, but a new one that widens at the horizon. If there are three men in the subway accompanied by a very small child, I can't think of anything else, I hope they are doing that child nothing but good. I leave them and next I observe a woman bent over a piece of paper, who doesn't seem to be writing anything at all. I go home, and across the street I observe a little boy who has been left alone. And just then you fling yourself at my back, you love me and that's why you imitate what you call supreme happiness. I have a friend named Jeanne and I want things to be good for her, I want her son to grow up, I want us all to be there twenty years from now. All that I put in a big envelope that is never out of my sight, that breathes at night at the foot of my bed.

I've composed that letter in my head a thousand times and on every page I wrote, There has to be a place to put our love, but in the end I never did it. I didn't know where to begin. I didn't know if you were supposed to use key words to divide things up. For example the park, songs, the castle filled with all the shapes of life. I didn't know what would matter most for Maria.

And here I am with this little girl who is almost four years old, who in years to come will have nothing to examine but a series of photographs, she'll pause at one of them and say, This looks like me, or, This one doesn't look like me, and nothing else will remain of her childhood, just a few remarks such as: I had funny hair, a funny sweater, I was laughing, and what can you see behind me?

4

Jeanne is here with her miniature camera and this is our opening scene: Jeanne and Gabriel walking into Albanie's and Maria's house. There are a few steps to climb and you can still see on the door the nail on which the Christmas wreath was hung.

Things continue to exist.

I open the door, I'm very good at that, I push Maria

into the living room because it's cold, Gabriel gives her a snowball that she's going to put in the freezerator, as she calls it.

On the floor in one corner of the kitchen sits a pile of Saturday papers that I'll never have time to read. In the middle of the living room stands Maria's circus, which we set up this morning. The elephants are holding yellow umbrellas, the animal tamers are training camels, and several little figures are holding musical instruments. They're all wearing hats with a feather, and bows on their necks, and Maria insists very firmly that they're girls even though they look like soldiers. Gabriel gives me a funny look, I say, It's true, they're all girls, and then I walk out of the camera's range.

A little later we go outside to play and for this sequence I'm the one holding the camera. The children are talking to the snow and Jeanne stays close to them, not moving. Now everything on the planet seems immobile.

My neighbour across the street is walking her baby in its stroller through the living room. We can see her silhouette bending over slightly, then she straightens up and waves at me.

Felix is watching us from his living-room window. There is no one in the rocking chair, no shadow.

Suddenly he disappears for a few minutes, then reappears wearing his tuque, coat, and mittens. He comes outside to join us and we see right away that his boots aren't done up. Jeanne kneels down to tie them. He says, Daddy go bye, like an eighteen-month-old child. It's as if he's apologizing, and I am more and more convinced that he is now part of our life.

Now Jeanne is filming me while I talk on the phone.

Maria's father asks me what time he should come for her tomorrow. I turn around, I don't want her to see the thing trembling inside me.

On Sunday she films me alone in my bedroom. I open the closet door and show her the marbles in my shoe. I've left them there. Like the nail on the door. Because that is how the world turns and things continue to exist.

5

We're dancing to a Liza Minnelli song. I'm waving my arms and I appear to be wearing a sweater that's cut very low in the back. But I'm not. I'm wearing a big red sweat-shirt, I've taken off my jeans and my socks have fallen down around my ankles. If anyone passing by looks in the window, they'll think I've lost my mind.

I'm at Jeanne's house.

We've looked at what we have filmed so far. There's so much snow we feel as if we're living in an igloo. That shows what's on our minds. An igloo where all of us can sleep together. This is how it happens, we're all together on a little white street, and outside this moment life is ter-rifying on several faces of our many-sided hearts.

In Jeanne's living room the walls are all yellow. A huge photograph of a very black tree cut at an angle hangs on the wall. I sit under the tree and tell stories.

The first is about a man who ate an airplane. He started with the wings, then went on to the screws, the dials, and all the metal. His legs got heavier and heavier until, ten years later, he died. Now his legend is in one of the most-read books in the world.

Jeanne nods her head, she's filming objects scattered on the rug, then more objects, then the emblem of every-thing here that will die, and then she turns back to me.

The second story is about intentional immobility. A man named William A. Fuqua didn't move for four and a half hours. It was nothing new for him, he was a model. This time though he wasn't posing, he was accomplishing a feat. He couldn't know that later he would be stabbed in the back by a man who wanted to prove something to his wife: to show that Fuqua was nothing but a doll. But the man was mistaken. That's a true story, one that conceals other stories, and since that time the two men have been united in the same sentence, in the same book, forever.

I can't get the sentence out of my head. By them-selves, these accounts would not exist. It's the sum of these sentences that turns them into an exploit and at the same time presents us with an alarming image of the world. A monstrous one.

For me, it's like that every day: I'm at work, a little tired, horrified at the stories that emerge from the walls. There are full days and there are empty ones, like these. They're the worst because you can never fill them with meaning, you can't put words into them and then plunge into reflection. You can only talk about what has been and what otherwise will never be.

We entitle this scene: Sunday afternoon. Jeanne puts up her hair at the mirror. We clean the glass table. I stop for a moment. I see someone dying. In the film there are no odours; but in memories and in the future, there are. Even in books, a little, at least I think so.

When I go home I draw a tree for Maria and under it I write "tamarack."

I could add this: I spend my time observing everything, and everything stays inside me. The forest is so dense, Maria. And it dwells inside me. Tonight, for example: I mustn't get up even if I hear a murmur in your bedroom. I know that voice. It's the voice of a child who is crying and it stays inside me. I must not get up. I must spend this evening quietly, alone, while you aren't there, I mustn't look out the window.

I am here, Maria.

I can talk on the phone and tell someone, Hello, I'm here. I can draw a tamarack tree and even discover a city that doesn't appear on any map. But I cannot show what is deep down in my heart.

6

Now that she knows I saw her from my window, Maria hasn't been so frightened at daycare. She no longer puts her hands over her ears, she's learning lots of songs that I don't know.

When she leaves in the morning she takes a little fetish: a candy she keeps in her pocket, the picture of the glacier, or the picture of me that she usually keeps under her pillow.

When she goes to Grandma's she doesn't take anything. She says that she has all her things there, she says my things, and my picture continues to sleep under her pillow.

She says she had a nightmare dream at Daddy's.

What was it about?

Nothing, it was just a dream that had nightmares in it.

If memories have odours so do dreams, and they can turn into nightmares.

It's a kind of emotion. We are simply sitting around a table. Our whole family is there. We're having a conversation and at a certain point we shrink, and then we wake up crying. And for the rest of the day we try to eliminate that emotion. That odour.

As for Maria, I don't know. She laughs when she says the word nightmare. Sometimes she stops playing and asks me to come and comfort her.

I comfort her.

Even if I don't know the reason.

That's something her father could never do for me. Or any other man, for that matter. When we cry we have to take a kind of examination, we have to explain why, and if we pass it we're entitled to be held in their arms.

When they leave us we pass the examination easily. We know how to say, Don't go away, we know how to say Please, we even know how to sit down and write a letter. Our hand trembles a little and at that moment, when we're on the threshold, we're entitled to a little love. Later, on the same threshold, it's often their turn to want to say something. But they don't say it and the deeds remain.

This morning another little girl arrived at the daycare in tears. Her name is Jessica. Maria watches her out of the corner of her eye, she moves away, she doesn't want to talk to her at all.

At the end of the day she leaves without saying good-bye.

She answers the phone, she tells Jeanne that there's a little girl who cries, but it's not Maria.

7

The following weekend we continue to work on our film. Whenever we're outside the house Felix comes over and joins us. He helps us build an igloo.

Occasionally he'll say something that is going through his head: My snowsuit is blue, I ate some gum. He manages to avoid saying many of the words with the letter R in them. He doesn't say cereal, he doesn't say rock or cry, but we can guess them. Like him, we know the power of words.

Once his father opens the window, he sticks his head out and yells at Felix to stop bothering us. I say, No, he isn't bothering us. He looks at me very hard and says, Yes he is.

You'd have thought he wanted to kill me.

I don't know why I do it, but I do, I put down my shovel, I head for their front door, open it, walk into the apartment, I see three rooms that are almost empty—a double living room with a bed, a sofa, the rocking chair and a TV set, a kitchen at the back, and a bedroom, Felix's room, where all I can see are a bed and a little bookcase with trucks and puzzles and some model figures on the shelves.

I sit on his bed, I try to understand, and then I go back outside.

The man is still sitting in his chair. He doesn't look at me. He's trying to imagine a wall around himself and that wall is his anger at me.

I try to ask him what's going on with Felix and of course the words come out wrong. They no longer have power.

Then the man gets up, grabs my arm, and pushes me out of his apartment.

Outside, nothing has happened. Felix has been more successful than his father at erecting a wall to protect himself. Behind it he sees only the snow, the igloo, Gabriel and Maria.

She asks me what I saw in Felix's house.

Some nice puzzles, Maria.

Then she wants to know if we'll be going there for supper.

She has put on her pink pajamas with the hearts, and over them her mauve skirt, and then her pink socks with the stars. She got dressed by herself, to surprise me.

She says we'll have to find a new dress for Salome.

I ask her if she loves me. She says yes, and then she goes to pack her suitcase for our trip to the North Pole.

I hold her very tight because I love her, because I know she never forgets anything.

8

We've put a new sentence on the refrigerator door. It's about the Far North and it says: *Currently, geographical north corresponds fairly precisely with the direction of the North Star.*

We like that sentence and ever since it's been there, in our kitchen, we spend a lot of time examining it from every angle. We imagine the colour of each word: when we say "north," we see our white footprints in the snow.

I explain to Maria that it can be green there too, it can be summer in some places with yellow flowers and pink ones, and the glaciers stand out against the blue sky before us.

It is certain now that we're going there. We must leave

our dream book and enter reality with just a few clothes in our suitcase. The air will have a quality that only we will comprehend. It will be our memory. A pure white memory, like our footprints in the snow.

I haven't seen Felix's father again, but we've noticed something new behind the window.

A woman went into their living room holding a little package. She sat on the arm of the sofa and Felix started running around in every direction. He circled her because she was hiding the package under her coat. She showed it to him and then she unwrapped it while he watched.

We didn't see what it was but Felix was happy, he was laughing. Then they both went out, and the next day Felix was once again a sad little boy on the stairs.

Today, Maria wants to know if Felix is her friend and how you play with a friend.

She says, How do you imitate an avalanche, Mummy? How do you play with the North Star?

I tell her, You put it right there, in front of you, and then you imagine all the mountains you have to cross to reach it.

Will we always be here?

I say, Yes, we'll always be here.

But tonight in my bedroom that certainty is gradually disappearing.

9

It is an uninhabited room.

Inside it something is happening, I don't know what. I hear that voice, something is happening, something is happening, but I can't understand what it is.

I can't see anything.

Just that sense of danger, of boundaries overstepped, of walls that are caving in.

I write those sentences under the words "to live" and they are also, I believe, a definition of "to witness."

What do we witness, Maria? And what do we two witness, Jeanne? Have we ever been at the bedside of a dying woman, have we ever bent over her to hear what is left of her voice tell us that she is afraid, afraid of what she sees, afraid of dying and of being all alone in death? Have we ever looked at the underside of a life?

And Agnes, what happened to plunge her into that silence of hers, what has she witnessed that has made her a woman who sits at the same table every day, making the same gestures, opening books and studying the pictures for a sign?

And Felix?

In Jeanne's video we are people wearing mittens, the bigger ones have bands over their ears that pull their hair up, the smaller ones have hats that are firmly tied under their chins.

You can see quite clearly what is timid about us, you can see the sky that sucks us up, and the little boy who stands off to the side.

Sadness too is off to one side, it won't kill us. Perhaps it's a sign in the book Agnes is holding now. Or that letter I've never written. But it won't kill us.

Mittens.

At the daycare this morning there was a sheet of paper stuck to Felix's locker. I went over to it and read: "Can you please give Felix some mittens to wear? And underpants too, if possible? We could teach him how to

keep himself clean and that would give him a more posi-
tive self-image."

I helped Maria to undress. I took my time, even more
than usual. I didn't leave right away because I had to talk
with Lise. And just then we witnessed something we'll
never be able to put out of our minds.

We saw Felix, a little boy three years old, walk into
the daycare alone. He came here all by himself, he waited
for someone to come up behind him and open the door, he
turned left in the corridor of this old school, then he
found his class and went in.

He saw the paper stuck to his locker but he didn't say
anything.

The event occurred, and like all events it will continue
to occur, elsewhere, and without us. But starting with this
one here, we'll begin to know a few things about Felix.

Lise said, Now it's up to me to act.

I hugged Maria just a little too hard. No, sadness won't
kill us, but it does make us hug those we love too hard.

I kissed her, twice instead of once, and for the rest of
the day nothing really happened to me.

10

At the bird feeder at my father's house a bluejay is hun-
grily eating seeds.

Through the lens of a camera we can see it arrive and
start eating with jerky movements of its little blue head,
stop now and then to look around, begin again, stop, then
fly away towards the horizon.

Maria asks if it has a mummy: that's her way of putting
some order into the universe.

Later, when the bird comes back with what seems to

be its mummy, she wants to know if it has a daddy.

And so it is, for all things.

Mummy, am I a little bird?

Last night she tore up a piece of paper and told me, Look, I'm tearing up your anger.

I didn't think she could sense my anger. And I didn't know if that was really what was inside me—anger had turned up here like a stray kitten.

I was sitting in the black chair, simply sitting there because there was nothing else I could do.

I was thinking about the news report on one of the horrors of Romania under the Ceaucescus, the children abandoned in an institution, heads shaven, naked, covered with excrement, and with some kind of worms crawling over their legs. I watched as they clung to one another, while I simply sat in my black chair.

This time I turned off the TV and at her house Jeanne did the same, because we couldn't bear any more.

I was sitting there, exactly as I was last night, and I was digging tunnels we could escape through. I couldn't move because I was torn between two people: the one with Maria, work, happiness, the black chair, and another Albanie who went across the street and bashed the door in, who picked up little Felix at the very least, and took him away with her forever.

It wasn't anger but a kind of annihilation, because I couldn't establish any connection between the two Albanies. It's always the same problem—connections, the connections that we can't establish, that we ought to make between things, between slow, profound assassination and life which is a promise made to my little Maria.

Lise said there was nothing I could do for the time being.

My mother listens to me talk about Felix. She recognizes the way I feel. In particular, she knows it affects others. We are calmly eating in the dining room, then we change the subject and listen to what Maria has to say.

There's a watercolour facing us: the sea, and trees laden with fruit.

The little bluejay has flown back towards the horizon.

And we aren't birds, Maria. No one really takes us under their wing, even if we still believe at first that we're the most loving creatures in the world. We believe we're twins: we go to sleep with our brother or our sister, and then one day we're like a budgie bird that dies of sadness because its mate is gone. But it only lasts for a while. We do not die.

No one kills us for that.

11

She tells my father, I want to see when my mummy was a child.

My father pulls open a drawer and takes out several reels of film. They're so old, it can't be me.

A few minutes later, a little girl four years old is strolling along the sidewalk. She's wearing a pink dress of honeycomb cotton. Ahead of her is a little sister who is just beginning to walk.

It's hard to recognize the street because of the trees that are not yet trees.

The little girl is an actress, she positions herself in front of the camera and offers her smile for eternity.

She knows.

It's one of the things children know.

After that, another moment in the day. She's going up and down the stairs. Once to the left. Once to the right. Her hair is in braids and she's dressed in green corduroy slacks and a blue blouse. She seems to be asking, Like this?

Then we see her outside, through the living-room window. There are no curtains. She's laughing. She's wearing a strange hat with buttons on one side.

Maria says, She looks like a rabbit.

Now my mother explains to her about the years without curtains, the park outside the house, the children who threw stones. The trees have grown. On the beach, a mother sits next to her child, reading. The child is burying her little white feet in the sand. The sky changes and they both look up. The child is thinking about a bag of candies on the counter, and the mother is wishing she could no longer see the future before her. Later, the scene starts up again with a more precise (or more restricted, it depends on the individual) sense of the years, especially the present that is no longer merely present.

There it is, I was happy, and now Maria is asking if she and I laugh that much in our film. The next episode seems to her like a dream in which I'm laughing as I hold her out at arm's length.

I'm sure that my mother and I are thinking the same thing when we ask Maria, What would we do without you?

We are thinking about everything that goes on behind a window without curtains, about the time that has passed so quickly, the time that has built, so slowly, all manner of corridors and trap doors to welcome us. We are thinking, Maria is there, until finally we are no longer the focus of the story. We are growing older, and every day some extraordinary phrase reveals our soul.

Maria has taken out her set of china dishes to serve us coffee. She mimics us, asks very politely if I'd prefer a glass of wine.

I look at my mother and want to tell her, I just hope I don't lose all my teeth, so Maria won't see me in a coffin with my mouth sewn shut.

But I say, I'd prefer a glass of wine and, I'm going to have to find a school.

My mother says, Already?

Already.

I tell her about Felix again, about Jeanne, and about our forthcoming trip to Alaska.

12

We will never know why coincidences shake us up, or why a story spins around us and then one day lands at our feet. All we do is understand a little, just a little, the themes that haunt us. For example, we finally understand what we were looking for as children, in the middle of the night. What fell on the floor, what we picked up and held tight in our arms. We put on a heavy pullover and fall asleep in a sweat, because it's summer and it's much too warm.

It was while thinking about what I couldn't do for the majority of children that I put the Block Parent sign in my living-room window. I couldn't know that at that very moment a coincidence was turning up at my door.

Right after I'd put up the poster I heard the bell ring. I opened the door and there stood someone I didn't know, who asked me, Is this your child? His voice dripped contempt, but it doesn't matter. All that matters is that I saw Felix standing on the sidewalk in front of my house and crying. The person said, He's been crying like that for an hour at least. So then I picked up Felix in my arms and took him with me.

I tried to calm him but there was nothing to be done, he was crying so hard that his whole little body was trembling.

I put him in Maria's bed and each of us held his hand until he calmed down.

Maria gave him her cat with the bell to hold, she stroked his hair and he fell asleep like that.

I called Jeanne and asked, What should I do?

Nothing, she said, nothing. I'll go see if his father's at home.

He wasn't, of course.

Felix was still asleep when Jeanne arrived. The two of us talked and then a little later we heard Maria's voice. She was speaking to him. Softly. Very softly.

We gave them something to drink and all he said was that his father had gone away and that it was too long to be outside all by himself.

There was a key in his pocket and we wondered how a three-year-old would be able to open a door with a key. Connections again. We were completely baffled because we didn't know what could connect this act with a three-year-old child.

Then I heard the bell: it was his father, and all he said was, Where is he?

I can still see them. When they walk past the window his father notices the sign and a terrible weight seems to land on his shoulders. Felix is walking behind him, his eyes are puffy but it doesn't matter, he no longer thinks he's all alone. They go home and we are left with that image.

13

How can a single act make us experience someone else's day? Putting a sign in the window, observing a bird, or looking at yourself in the mirror and discovering a wrinkle that doesn't go away. It's because we're thinking about someone else's acts and the meaning of all life is precisely there, in the fact that our acts are at the same time always those of someone else.

For Felix, this is what happens. We stood there for a long time, looking at his footprints behind his father's, signs of his forgiveness. From time to time Gabriel and Maria occupied a place in his body, because his sorrow contained all sorrows. Then another act swelled up inside us: putting a hand on the child's forehead, tracing the line of his eyebrow with our fingers, closing our eyes and concentrating so that he'd fall sleep.

Jeanne left and we fixed supper, like thousands of other people in the city.

After her bath, a perfectly clean, smooth Maria came and clung to me, and then another coincidence took charge of us. There was a report on television about the return of the sun to Inuvik, north of the Arctic Circle. People were gathered around a fire, waiting for the night to pass and the sun to reappear. They hadn't seen it for a month and that was why, on the night in question, the sun was a god behind the clouds. The people were talking about light as they held the hands of their wide-eyed children.

This time, because of the clouds, the sun didn't really appear until three days later. We saw it rise and then a few minutes later it went down again, like a hand stroking a head. A flock of people came after it, dancing, and everyone was wearing dark glasses. It was their celebration, a beginning of the world, because they knew that now the sun was going to stay a little longer each day, until June, when it would come to stay for sixty days.

Maria told me she wanted to go there. She added, And bring Felix too. And then we became two small children in their coats, with fur around our faces.

We went to her room and that image managed to insinuate itself into me.

I watch her sleep.

Her sleep may be united with a dream, or with the desire of another person, in another house. It may be a glassy lake beside a mother who turns her head away. That mother remembers a caress by the man who is no longer part of her life. His caress retains her still. She stays seated, she puts her hand on her daughter's arm. She reassures herself that it is her child, that she does exist and she is not an unloved little boy. She looks at her and touches her again. She stands up. The next day, a single little wrinkle swings her at once into the past and the future. It is the nucleus of her life.

14

In my dream the smallest interchangeable being is lying across Maria's bed.

The closer I am, the more anonymous I become.

I am no longer sitting between two Albanies, I catch up with the acts that were waiting for me by telling the little creature over and over: *Words are so simple.*

What I mean is that underlying any question, the answer is always whatever is simplest.

The first time we examine the question closely, we find nothing, or only a few murmured words that are practically silence.

The second time, we forge a complex answer with networks and ramifications.

But if we continue to go deeply into the question, we find an answer that is even simpler than the first.

That answer is the one we need, it's the little light that glows behind each of our deeds.

In Jeanne's video, we can see joy now, and that joy creates a shadow on the wall. It comes away and turns into a precious thing that we keep hidden in our hand, inside our mitten, like a bus ticket.

Here are the planets that gravitate around us: some red-stone houses, each with an outside staircase for going in and out, a fruit and vegetable stand, a Fisher-Price garage, a giant atlas, a doll named Zaza who is always lying on the floor under the bed, books, a box that holds a seashell, two mismatched earrings and a hairpin, a crystal turtle that sparkles and holds a memory too, a lot of photographs, a pile of clothes, a dream book.

Maria looks at the map and asks again where we are. She strikes the pose of someone who is mulling things over, then she says, I have a lot of things to watch today.

On the video we don't see Salome, the little imaginary entity who lies on the couch to be undressed and taken care of.

Maria puts a compress on her forehead. She says, You'll feel better, you'll see.

Across the street, my neighbour rocks her baby, she

lays him in his bed, then she lies down too and leafs through a magazine. She reads an article about a princess and her heirs, then she comes upon the story of the lost twins who find each other again. She shuts the magazine and imagines which of the details in that story could be addressed to her. She closes her eyes. She smiles. She falls asleep.

We're here, Maria.

Universal Attraction

I said it is the nucleus of her life. What I meant was, the nucleus of her being. What is inside the nucleus of each being? It may be something very small. Hidden shoes, a child toddling along behind an image. A deed, a single deed that has never been done. A hotel room with white sheets. A phrase. A spray of light. A whistling sound.

This nucleus is what connects us to the earth; it makes us stand on the ground and hold out our arms, each in our own way, towards another person. It is the simplest response to all our questions.

As for Felix, we already know what will always be inside him: a small child toddling along behind his father. The man does not turn around. Alone, the little boy goes on crying.

We've taken three days off. Maria is so happy that she doesn't see the core of fatigue inside the house. That's the reason. I have to lie on the sofa while she watches "La Bande à Ovide," she shouts that she loves the blue duck, and then she comes and lies on top of me so that I'll give her permission to do it all.

To do it all means to watch the same programme ten

times over while she drinks juice and eats whatever she wants.

When the phone rings Maria picks it up and says, We're exhausted.

She says we're going to have a party while we wait for spring, like the one they have at Inuvik for the sun. She looks for her sunglasses and walks around the house singing. She doesn't want to invite anyone else, just the two of us, and there won't be any candles.

She's only three and a half. I have to stop everything and organize this party now, because afterwards it will be too late. There won't be any more real holidays. Afterwards she'll have to take her place in a time that doesn't include us, she'll have to be pulled by the sleeve, she'll have to take the bull by the horns, and plunge. But what we really need, and that's the reason for our fatigue, this core of fatigue, this three-day holiday, is love. We must love. That's all, it's always too much, it's everything.

Today for the first time I felt a warm, light wind when I opened the door. I told Maria, We're going out, and we went to look at the Easter window at the bakery.

The sky is clear. We've stowed all our sadness in the cupboard because the weather is fine. We look at one another, a little surprised by the good luck of this isolated day, and we wait for the change to appear on our faces.

Maria knows what has to be done.

She blew a kiss to the little chocolate Kalimaro in the window and made me promise to come and get him. The little duck has a checkered scarf on his head and Maria explains that he's an orphan too. She means like Rémi, Tchao, Boumbo, Salome, like almost all the children she knows.

On the way home she stops in front of the house. She asks if we can sit on the steps because it's so beautiful. She's looking for something in the air, she shouts because what she's looking for is precisely there, in the air all around us.

I sit beside her and immediately I discover this scene inside me: Agnes is sitting on the library steps reading a letter, a tear runs down her cheek but she doesn't appear to be crying; she seems to be holding the air, the warm wind, in her hands.

Maria has put her head on my knees.

We close our eyes, like Agnes, and like her we keep the warm wind in our hearts, we are that wind, this street, this moment.

2

Madame Raymond is a woman dressed in navy blue whose reason for living is to be found somewhere inside the library. My own reasons for living can be found anywhere but here.

Sometimes when I stop at the letter M and come upon *The Member of the Wedding* I am truly present, here in this library, inside a sentence or the entire book. That is all and it can't last very long.

Agnes is the only person with whom I have a connection, because I don't know who she is and because she's part of my dreams. Because her hands tremble, and because deep inside her there is something she can't do. There's a lake in which she can't drown herself.

When I go in, Madame Raymond always nods to me. Her nod is the image of perfection. She does it to show me, along with her own relevance, what she sees reflected in the way I look: a double room where the books are incorrectly classified, where things never stay in place, where I am sometimes lying down and covered by a crowd of people and things.

That act is performed by a woman who gently sets down on the counter a purse that matches her shoes. She takes out a sheet of paper on which are entered the days I've been absent. She tells me to pay a little more attention. Perfect.

Agnes looks at me and smiles. Today her hair is a little more blond and she's happy. She smiles, for me and then for herself. She has removed her bracelets and set them on the table. No books. Just the sun beating down on her neck.

Jeanne has come to pick me up for lunch. We go to the most out-of-the-way table and Jeanne pulls a snapshot of Gabriel from her wallet. The waitress winks at us: the child's picture in Jeanne's wallet is our connection with her. Her wink says that things are the same, they'll never change.

We've learned that someone is finally going to see about Felix. He's not a battered child in the usual sense of the term, but Lise has gathered enough information for something like an investigation of his case.

We talk about him for almost an hour.

We hold our faces in our hands, sometimes Jeanne lights a cigarette, we look around us, but we always come back to the person who will gather up Felix and take him away from his house.

How will we know if he's all right, if his pajamas smell of soap, if he gets lots of kisses at bedtime? How will we know, when his birthday comes, if he's glad to be four, if he can be a big boy of four and talk and play and do silly things like a child of four?

Jeanne puts her hand on my arm. It means that I will never be that person.

I know.

Then, before we leave, she lowers her head and tells me she's seen Jacques again.

She lowers it just a little, for just a fraction of a second, but Jeanne's heart is in that gesture, and the unacceptable idea of desertion. Of Jeanne all alone, that is, deprived of the image that is sent to her by someone she once loved.

In self-defence she wraps her red scarf around her head and bursts out laughing.

In any case, love is an impossible thing.

That's what she says.

Now the waitress shows us a photo of her son. He's eighteen years old.

She looks so young when her eyes fill with tears.

Beside the picture of her son is one of a man who resembles him. His father.

She doesn't tell us who the tears are for.

She only says that time passes so quickly.

She wipes her hands on her apron.

It's true that love is a thing that's not possible on our planet.

3

When the waitress's eyes filled with tears I thought at once of Agnes. Hers are eyes that don't cry, but a tear falls from them out of habit. Even though Agnes smiled yesterday, every move she made continued to reveal an existential tragedy. Another one.

I looked for a sentence to express the things we'll never understand and I copied it onto a piece of yellow paper that I folded and stowed in my jacket pocket.

It read: *And the word* suffer *was one she could not associate with John Henry, a word she shrank from as before an unknown hollow darkness of the heart.*

I didn't put it up on the refrigerator door when I went home.

Maria is a genius. She won't apologize when she does something wrong, she knows I'm angry but an apology is out of the question. Instead, she makes a speech where ultimately everything turns against me and I have to go and shut myself in my room so I can laugh.

She knows the language and she knows a lot about me, much more than anyone else. More than her father, who had begun to forget quite a lot towards the end.

For instance, he no longer knew what time I finished work at the end of the day. He no longer knew that I hated being in bed all by myself. Or talking alone. Or eating.

Finally he left and I really was all alone when I did certain essential things. Maria could sense it. That was why she started to come and whisper words of love in my ear.

Tonight she said, out of the blue, that spiders aren't always bad. And then, that I'm not always alone as I told Grandma on the phone a while ago. That she's here with me. That there are two of us. And that Salome is here with us too.

She also says that I'm strong because I can carry piles of laundry.

It's true, Maria.

I am strong.

I carry piles of laundry. I pick up a little girl and carry

her upstairs. I watch the news and I see images of murders and collective mourning. Then I hear a woman talking about children who have never had anyone to welcome them home after school. I am strong and I listen and I think that the word suffer has nothing to do with John Henry. Cruelty isn't what we think it is.

Tonight it is she, Maria, who puts my head in her lap. She strokes my hair as I have so often done for her. As she has done for Felix. She tells me a story about Salome.

When is our next day off, Mummy?

She is stroking my hair, and now that she's doing so, we should be able to go away and leave everything as it is.

I mean that now, before the tragedy grows in the belly of the world, we should leave everything behind us, build a cabin, and wait for it to pass.

Because now is the time when we must be together.

Entirely together.

4

Chance really has a grip on us.

I hadn't realized before that Alaska, the frozen sea and ice floes, was part of Frankie Addams's dreams. Hers too. I've been reading the book at the library for months now and that coincidence didn't turn up till today.

It may be because the dreams aren't exactly the same. Frankie's brother is constantly in her dream and she's thrilled to think of him offering the Eskimos some of the homemade fudge she's sent him. All her reasons for living are in that dream: she sends fudge to her brother, he offers it to the Eskimos, then he gets married and now she's part of his wedding, a member, and she's no longer alone.

In our dream, Maria's and mine, there are already two

of us. Our desire stops at that, we are two and sometimes we're foolish enough to think we're alone on this earth, sitting on an ice floe, looking at a singular landscape, the frozen sea, glaciers, so many gigantic shapes of life.

That's not all. I sense that there is something else, that for the time being chance is still, but that it already knows the man who has just gone into the house across the street, where Felix lives.

And then just as he is pulling the door shut behind him Maria and I go out, it's like a movie, the two doors closing simultaneously, two gazes meet and the first thing we do is inevitably directed towards the other person.

The man sees us, consults a piece of paper he's taken from his pocket, screws up his eyes and looks at us again, then goes away.

That's all. He planted an idea, then he went away. And what it means is that he'll be back.

I'm sure of it.

That was why I took Maria in my arms, to show him that I'm strong and loving. I took Maria in my arms so that image would be clearly engraved in his memory. In contrast with what he found at Felix's house. So that life will be possible on this planet, and so that he'll come back.

That's all.

Maria starts yelling, I want off, as if I were a bus or a train or something that goes past in a landscape. She wants to go and see Felix, but when I say no she gets away from me and I catch up with her outside his house. Through the window we can see his father standing motionless by the rocking chair.

I say, See, Felix isn't there.

She says, Okay, and then, I don't like his daddy.

After that we walk in silence to the park. That too is a

sign. The silence. Exactly the same as in the unoccupied room that defines his life.

In this silence, a heart beats and a voice breathes events that we know nothing of.

5

All the men I've ever known made me pass an examination. The same for Jeanne. They see us as staid, quiet, reassuring women, and they spend a lot of their time trying to make that image coincide with the person standing before them.

We mustn't move, mustn't touch them too much. We have to take a deep breath and imagine ourselves on a terrace in Rome, with another man who is capable of putting his head against our neck, of biting, of swallowing our hair, all afternoon.

In the beginning, of course, Maria's father knew how to do those sorts of things, things that make us feel as if three hours is forever. In the beginning, everything happens just the way we want and the details don't matter too much. For example, the fact that they never really talk to us is something we only become aware of later, when we start to shake off the image of ourselves as a laughing girl on the terrace of a café.

With Alexandre I was so removed from that image, all I could show him was a weird girl with her pockets full of words. For me, things had already begun to turn inside out like a glove.

This time I don't know if the man I glimpsed across the street will be a man in my life, but I'm sure that with the image he has of me and my little girl in my arms, there won't be any false starts. Perhaps love is a thing that exists, but we are witnesses; we look straight ahead, we are witnesses, we do not laugh.

When he comes back a week later, it happens that we're outside again, we're walking past Felix's house just as he emerges, and right away Maria submits him to an examination. Things are turning inside out like a glove.

She asks him what he's doing. That's a big question and he replies that he looks after children.

Like me? asks Maria.

No, not like you. He smiles inside himself.

She says, Good, which means he's passed the first test.

He looks at me then and asks me, even though he already knows, if I am Albanie. He says that he's in charge of Felix's case, I say, In charge of? He says, Yes, in charge of, and in fact he'd like to talk to me about it.

Maria tugs at my sleeve, she insists on telling him that her name is Maria, what's yours?

Pierre, he says his name is Pierre.

Maria thinks it over.

Good. He's just passed the second test.

He waves to Maria, gazing at me with his rather sad green eyes. He says, See you later. Or, I'll call you, I don't remember which.

As I turn to go in the opposite direction an image comes back to me, that of marbles looking up at me against the black lining of a shoe.

I grab Maria by her waist, I say, I know what we're going to do, we're going to buy some shoes for spring.

I think, that way it will come faster. Spring, I mean. And all the rest. Everything will happen sooner.

6

Agnes has new shoes too. She turns up one morning in red shoes and a black dress and she tells me happily that it's spring.

This is the second time she has spoken to me. I'd like to ask her all sorts of things, details about her life, about David, but I hold back, saying only that it's still a little cold. She replies that she lives nearby and that's why she comes here every day. For the peace and quiet, she adds.

Now I can see where she lives. An old building on a boulevard.

Her apartment is filled with plants, and there are rugs everywhere that still smell of fire. You have to bend down towards the floor to smell it. Agnes does so often, she kneels and then she lies down on the Persian rug in the living room. She is one body with her past, utterly, she cannot separate herself from it.

All the objects in her house are souvenirs. Agnes runs her hand over her favourite knick-knacks.

Beside the sofa, a rattan table holds a bottle of orange liqueur and two crystal glasses. She picks up a glass, she pours the liqueur, looking closely at the little spots on her hand. With her other hand she tries to erase the spots. She is unaware that she is doing so. She turns on the radio. She waits for the evening to end. She has no one.

Agnes doesn't wear a wedding ring. She is sixty years old. She's alone. It's written on her face.

At the end of the day she speaks to me for the third time. Because it's spring or perhaps because of what she can read on my face. She asks if the little girl will be back soon. She's talking about Maria. I smile at her without replying.

Mine are yellow, very plain, with the kind of flat heel

that I like. Maria's are navy blue with a little buckle. We have put them at the foot of our beds.

Every night when we come home, we put them on. It's a kind of exercise. Maria says she has to explore them to be sure she likes them.

At Easter, then, we go to Grandma's, she in her blue-and-white striped dress and her little buckled shoes, and me in jeans as usual but with a yellow sweater, yellow shoes, amazing rococo lipstick.

Jeanne and Gabriel have been invited too.

Maria asks if there are lots of people and if it's a party.

Yes, there are lots of people and it's a party.

She draws what she calls a wonderful egg, for Gabriel. She says it doesn't matter, she used to not like parties but now she does. Now she's older and she understands.

Gabriel keeps talking about Jacques, he came over last night and brought him a Playmobil for his collection, an ice-cream seller, then he flung his arms wide open and Gabriel was so glad to see him again.

As for Maria, she can't stop talking about Salome who stayed behind in her room because she doesn't want to see anybody.

Jeanne talks about Jacques.

My father talks about birds.

My mother talks about childhood that's not something hidden in a closet.

A vision of Agnes, she is sitting down with a glass of brandy that trembles a little on her lap.

A vision of Felix, a woman brings him a little chocolate bunny. When she leaves, he throws it in the garbage.

A vision of myself, I cross the street, I take a man called Pierre by the arm, I don't finish a single sentence, I make him swear that he won't fall asleep before I do.

7

Today is a real holiday. Felix came over to play with Maria and I sat in my beach chair on the balcony to keep an eye on them.

He doesn't play well.

When Maria blows soap bubbles he doesn't know if he should laugh or catch them or simply stand back and watch.

He doesn't laugh. He holds his little hands in the air, not overdoing it, but not coming out of himself; it's as if he has no will, as if he has nothing to catch, but still everything depends on his doing this—holding out his hands to mark his lowly presence in this space.

After that Maria takes three little Easter eggs from her pocket, she offers him one and he turns to me as if to ask permission. I say, Take it, Felix, it's a present from Maria. He takes it, puts it in his pocket, and keeps checking to see that the egg is still there.

Later, at lunch time, he doesn't say goodbye, or anything. He stuffs his hands in his pockets and goes home.

Today, Pierre finally decided to come and talk to us. Maria has pulled her little chair up next to mine, we toss our heads back and we look as if we really are on a beach, or in an English garden, or on the verandah of a sanitarium. That's the effect we want. When he gets here our eyes are closed and all we hear is a slightly hoarse voice saying hello.

Maria calls out, Whew, we were scared, and immediately shows him her pocket filled with Easter eggs. He tells her she's a lucky girl and gently strokes her hair.

I'm glad he does that. It's like a kind of secret between us, something that is understood, the proper way to touch a child. I say, She's my little spring angel. He smiles and sits on the top step of the staircase. Very close to me. Very close to us.

He asks us some questions about Felix. He says that Lise mentioned me and said I might be able to help him form some idea. That's not altogether true though. His mind is already made up. He talks about Felix as an abandoned child, too small for his age, too timid, too lost. He says that the child's mother only comes to see him now and then, that it's worse when she does come, that his father is inconsistent, just that, inconsistent, that he has Felix looked after by no one in particular, and above all that no one at home ever talks to him. He watches television, he constructs a world for himself in which he can't be touched.

Pierre is looking down while he tells us. You might think he came here just for that, to look at the ground, to talk about what he sees there. At one point he looks up and says, The worst thing is that he's by no means the only one.

Then, I don't know why—nor does he, for that matter—he kisses Maria, kisses me, and leaves.

Perhaps I asked him to without realizing it, because I am looking for someone to complete certain gestures within me, and perhaps he is that person.

And perhaps the only look I gave him today was that one.

He leaves.

We stay there, planted in the sun.

8

Words continue to spring up around us. For instance there are tulips in the flower-bed. Red ones and yellow ones. And along with the tulips: bulb, stamen, pollen, leaf, etc.

Every morning Maria goes to see if they've opened. She wears a jean jacket over a red sweater now, and sometimes a little green tuque. When it's warm enough, the sun falls directly onto her hair, and it's as if the sun's rays are focused entirely on her.

Life is slower now. We dawdle on the street for a long time. We drop in often on Jeanne to sample a new mixture of exotic fruit juices. In the evening we add alcohol, sometimes a lot of alcohol. The children don't sleep, life is still slow, but it's upside down, like an ashtray that has spilled onto the carpet.

Jacques is spending more and more time with Jeanne. They maintain their separate houses but they're together now, more than before.

Jeanne and I know what that means. We invent reasons for certain things. We place mad, blind deeds deep in Jacques's heart, and when we look at his face we see them there. What we know, we hold inside us like a mocking planet. We are not in a radiant future. We are in the present, and we plant flowers in the yard, for our children.

Sunday afternoon. Maria is with her father till tomorrow. I don't mind, because I packed her suitcase more calmly than I usually do.

He said, Hello, Albanie. That was different from other times too.

Maria didn't cry. We waited until she had finished her drawing, which was a surprise for him. For her, what was most important was that we let her finish her drawing.

She sent me a kiss in the mail, then she told me I'd have to look after Salome while she was gone. That's another way she makes connections.

Now I've opened all the windows and the silence is

sweet because it's not a real silence. It's the silence of spring, of summer, and that makes all the difference.

What do I hear in that silence? The sound of living things.

In the winter that sound makes me bend towards the earth.

In summer, though, the windows open and the sound puts up an edifice that rises into the sky.

So here I sit, with the image of a many-storeyed building. On each storey lives a person, each person doing something I can visualize. Agnes turns the pages of a book, Jeanne develops some new photos, Maria is asleep close to her father. Each person, even Maria in her sleep, utters some word or phrase that I wish I could hear.

And what about Pierre, what is he doing? He's writing something new in Felix's file. For instance, that he came to daycare all alone again the other day. Adding that even so, he managed to describe his day. Three short sentences. Felix managed to say three short sentences.

And what if Pierre thought of us when he closed the file? If he decided to stroll over here, just to see me? What would happen then? Would I begin by asking about Felix? Would we talk about Maria who has gone to her father's? Would he turn his head to listen to the music wafting out through the living-room window? Would he say he liked it? Would he stay long enough for me to offer him some exotic fruit juice with a little rum?

The music coming through the living-room window is Bashung's *Pyromane*, and the person who turns to listen to it is me.

I know the words by heart, they're on my lips, and I look like a girl who is too quiet and who talks to herself. Her balcony is inhabited by invisible beings.

As I turn around to hear the music better, I've stopped thinking, I mean the building has vanished from my consciousness.

I stand up to get a beer, it's afternoon, it's sunny, and when I come back I see Pierre crossing the street on his way to see me.

Things happen, they create a sound, and sometimes they're even stronger than they are in our heads.

9

He says that he doesn't know why but he wanted to see us again. Both of us. He has grasped the image.

Our first topic of conversation is easy to find then: Maria's absence, her father, and everything that comes after. He turns away slightly to listen to the record that's playing in the living room all by itself. That's our second topic of conversation: music, the best record of the year, etc.

Then we talk about Felix. There is something new in his file: his parents have agreed to have him placed with a foster family. He uses the appropriate term: placed.

Immediately, I see the image of a paragraph about Felix in the newspaper: *Please give me a home. Parents who'll know how to put on my mitts, teach me words, point out the stars in the sky.*

While Pierre is telling me about his work I keep seeing that image, and I see him bending over children, his expression gentle and his hands in his pockets.

He is talking and it's too late for me not to become attached in one way or another, because he is talking, because sometimes the words seem to have been chosen just for me, because I see the picture we would make, Pierre and the two of us, some afternoon in a park.

The record is over. I tell him to wait a minute and I come back with two glasses of exotic fruit juice. I've put in a lot of rum.

If he had a little girl too, I'm sure I could fall in love with him, just like that, some afternoon in a park or on a terrace, because of one little thing he did, wiping his child's mouth, gently, while she was laughing.

He drinks his juice, he looks at me, and I no longer know whether I look sad or embarrassed, or simply like a girl resting on a balcony.

There is a moment of tension that goes on for an eternity. I mean, until the sun sets behind the house.

We went to the living room, then to the kitchen, then back to the living room again. We looked at photos and he chose the one in which I'm holding Maria in my arms, we're in the ocean, her eyes are incredibly blue, they aren't my eyes but I am her love and my whole body has unfolded to say so.

That's what attracted him right away, I think. From the way he looked at the photos, you knew he was thinking that being the mother of a little girl is something lucky, that it formed a totality he wanted to take in his arms—that luck, me, Maria, and the love that flows between the two of us.

I'm not imagining that, it's something that exists even if it's rare. Even if we can never know what will happen afterwards. He grasped the image because he wanted it, wanted it at that very moment.

Just as the sun went down behind the house he came over to me and did what I'd been waiting for him to do. He ran his hand over my face like a blind man, then went on to the back of my head, to the nape of my neck, all over my back, finally he kissed my neck while he held me a little too hard; it was his way of saying goodbye, of drowning, of leaving me alone and drowning too, there in the middle of the living room.

10

That doesn't stop the mocking planet from describing its orbit around my heart. I hold onto it, it's inside me like another Albanie who's looking through a telescope. Everything resembles a car mirror that says: Caution, objects in mirror are closer than they appear. Albanie knows what is real. She can't get along without it. Not any more.

When I was recovering from drowning I saw the empty rum bottle on the floor and I started to laugh at myself. You should always do that.

I said all right, don't get worked up.

I poured a bottle of perfume on my neck, that was my immediate desire, then I ate a bowl of cereal and watched the news.

And that is how love begins, with desire personified, a bowl of cereal, and a night when we sense the presence of someone in our bedroom.

The next day Agnes is waiting for me at the library door with flowers. White lilies. She says, This is to brighten the day.

I say, It's true, it smells of rotten wood here. I open the door with Madame Raymond's keys. She isn't here this morning. The space is entirely reserved for me.

Till noon, I sit behind the counter with Agnes's flowers. Every time the door opens the wind accentuates the perfume of the lilies, and my heart sinks. I'm afraid it will be him. I don't want that. Not right away.

At noon the door opens, and it's Madame Raymond. I go to lunch by myself, like a big girl. Agnes never eats. I don't understand what makes her tick.

Life is a rare coincidence. An example: today. It's not my birthday or anything, but it seems as if the word is out. At ten to five the door opens, and it's Maria with her father behind her. A surprise for me. I won't have to go to pick her up at daycare. Her little suitcase is in the car. And then when I arrive at the house I see Jeanne and Gabriel sitting on the steps. She was waiting for me too. When she sees me get out of the car she has a funny look on her face. Maria's father waves to her. He kisses Maria, then he leaves.

As I'm walking into the house the phone rings, it's my mother wanting to know if everything's all right. Everything is all right. Come and talk to her, Maria.

Of course Jeanne is curious. She wants me to tell her everything, as usual, and I can't think of anything to say except that my stomach aches. I mean, it makes my stomach ache that life is a rare coincidence today. Because I'd like to be alone with Maria. Because I slept badly last night. Because I don't want the extreme tension that turns the minutes into eternity to become a sign of waiting. And because that's the way it is. Inevitably.

On her way out Jeanne sticks her head in the doorway and says, You see, in the end we always make a fresh start.

It's ten o'clock when the phone rings again.

The first thing he says is, I waited till you'd put her to bed. And so we all seem to have been waiting for something today.

11

I'm not afraid of love, or of being abandoned. I'm afraid of loving too much and of walking home at night when my sentences have fallen over a precipice and then been picked up.

Things were different with Maria's father. I didn't even feel like talking. I would look at his green running shoes and tell myself: that is him. Everything was understood, like in music, and I never came home alone at night. He was there, he accompanied me, he wasn't afraid either. What happened after that, long after, had nothing to do with love.

With all the others, my sentences ended up falling over a precipice.

And now.

Now I don't talk to him about the pain that has nothing to do with John Henry, I don't tell him about our trip or the dream book, I don't utter the word fear, I don't talk about the road, about suitcases, about the distance and the infinite connections that exist between things. I just tell him where to dig with his hands, where to find the images and even the emblem of desire.

I'm speaking generally.

While he, he looks inside.

Every night he calls me and we add more details, faces, memories.

After a week, a door in the library opens and he's there. He finds me at the back of the room, with the magazines.

I'm not protected, I'm there.

When he arrives I'm not sitting on a bench and waiting for him somewhere else, because I'm expecting him. I stand there, my hand on my back, I am absolutely there.

Besides that, as soon as I see him I smile, and that expands the space, the time, even the silence.

There are three individuals in that space. There's Agnes, now she's the one who's looking. I smile, time expands and touches Agnes. She's looking.

As for me, I calmly replace a magazine on the shelf.

He puts his hand in the pocket of my jeans, he touches my thigh, and leaves there a scrap of paper with a date and an address on it.

I think of the words "a week later" and I kiss him on the mouth.

Later, just before leaving, I go and sit next to Agnes.

At first she doesn't say anything, she holds her hands. Then she says, I've never been married, but love, yes.

I take the scrap of paper from my pocket to show her. He has drawn a house and on the door he has written, Will you and Maria come for supper?

Today is Friday. We are going to say yes.

12

We get out our new shoes and Maria's dress.

In the subway there is a woman who resembles a figure on an Etruscan vase. A long nose, a well-drawn head. Maria can't take her eyes off her.

Three stations go by and Maria stands up, she goes over to the woman, touches her arm to see if she's real. It's like a danger signal: the woman immediately turns around towards me. Seen full face, she still seems like a profile.

She looks at me.

I think: It's at times like this that things should reveal themselves.

A woman who's angry at Maria takes it out on me and I don't feel like telling her off or killing her or anything. I barely see her.

Maria says, Look, she's like a statue, and our presence rises into the air as usual.

But what stops me from seeing the woman as anything but a portrait on an Etruscan vase, what stops me from getting up and tossing off some killing remark, is a slight nervousness, like when you're expecting a surprise. I mean, what reveals itself is the photo of Pierre, which superimposes itself on the other images, and that's how I know that I'm beginning to love. To love someone other than Maria. Someone other than her father. I look at the woman who is looking at Maria and I do nothing, because at this very moment I know that I'm beginning to love.

Then Maria climbs onto me and she too launches into another subject: When I was little, I used to do this. Then she puts her nose against my cheek and sniffs me like a cat.

She's got it wrong. I'm the one who used to do that. I was always sniffing her, and it was fantastic to be stuck so close together, like two little animals who forget everything else.

We laugh. The woman watches us, her anger growing.

Fortunately, we get out at the Vendôme station, and when we arrive at Pierre's there are no more ordeals for us.

When we're inside Maria rushes into the kitchen and wants to know if there are any toys here. She says, You haven't got any sentences on your refrigerator. She adds, I've got a funny mummy.

Pierre tells her yes, and the way he says it sets me ablaze inside. It's a yes that encompasses everything, and that everything is clothed in desire. I rummage in my pockets because I don't know what to do. Things continue to reveal themselves.

While we're eating, there isn't a moment's silence. First because we've brought Carmel's cassette and Maria explains why we like it so much: her voice, her songs, and the way she moves her arms and smiles, closing her eyes and singing as if the world were an exceptional story that was suddenly being offered to her. We listen with our eyes closed, obliged to be like her because her song becomes our song too.

Then she tells him about our lives.

This is what is happening now, I mean since fate led Pierre to emerge from Felix's house at the same time we were leaving ours. Without seeming to, she describes our life, and now we are filling Pierre's head so that he'll be obliged to fall in love with us. That's the reason for Carmel's cassette, so that he'll be imbued with what we are always singing in our heads. So that he'll have a clear picture of what we're like. That's the reason for the shoes. The sentences on the refrigerator door. Things that don't exist, except for the two of us. Words in the dictionary. Language. Our entire territory.

She recounts our life. She doesn't know where it begins and where it ends, or why there is a North Pole in our dreams. She says, Mummy's beautiful. It's an examination question. And Pierre looks at me and says, Yes, and this time desire is inscribed there for good.

13

Maria tells Salome, Somebody's stroking Mummy's hair. She turns to me with her little nighttime expression and asks if we can bring Salome next time. Of course, Maria.

We came home late and Maria is too tired to sleep. So am I. I put my arms around her, I lie beside her, and here we are back in the igloo where we can see our shadows on the ice, where we can feel our breath, where we close our eyes and trace in our minds everything that happened today and everything that will happen tomorrow.

They tell us we should let our children cry in their beds. But they don't tell us how to do it. Or how to wake up in the morning and see the person we love most in the world lying at the foot of our bed, or on the floor against our bedroom door, how to look at that and put a key in our heart and say, Look, this is one of the rules of life.

Maria will soon be four and I've never known how to say that to her. All through her childhood there will be someone who goes to sleep after she does.

I told Pierre that and once again his hands crossed the distance between us.

He took my head in his hands and I could see his, his brown head, the long, curly hair, I saw his shoulders, his back, and all the rest in one glance, as if he were exploding in my heart; he took my head and he said, What's important is to love her, and he said that because he knew.

When we left, he whispered in Maria's ear, Your mummy is funny and she's beautiful too, and she smiled, smiled just a little, for herself.

In the taxi, she got up on her knees to look out the back window and she told me, Mummy, we're having a lot of nice days. The driver looked at us in the rear-view mirror and said, She speaks well for her age. Then, that he had a daughter too, twenty years old, and that when he wasn't working and she came home late he would sit on the living-room sofa and wait up for her. You'll see, it never ends.

That's not true. There is an end to every age, to every hour too, and one day I won't know anything about her. Hardly anything. In the meantime, I must do everything I can to know her.

I told Pierre that. He held me in his arms.

Tonight I'm sure that his presence will last in my bedroom until morning.

14

The windows are open. When people come to see us in the summer we hear them before they cross the threshold. If we're out in the yard, they come through the lane and peer through the gap in the fence to see if we're home. They open the gate, they see the flowers that Maria and I have planted, they see the two of us sitting on the Mexican blanket with a picnic, pieces of a jigsaw puzzle, magazines, and the white ankle-socks that we've just pulled off.

Maria knows the names of all the flowers. This is something fabulous in her language, in this city. She has taught me the names of the flowers we saw in the Italian part of town. Hollyhocks. And daisies.

It will be our birthday soon and now she is kneeling at the coffee-table, making decorations so the party will be decorative, as she says.

The windows are open.

Maria hears the footsteps first, heavy ones, a father's footsteps, they are climbing the stairs. Then slow steps, lighter ones, those of Felix.

We open the door and Felix rushes towards Maria's room. She follows him.

The father comes into the living room and asks if he can talk to me for five minutes. I say yes. But he doesn't say anything.

He just stands there in the middle of the living room. He looks around him. His hands hang on either side of his body.

From the bedroom we hear only Maria's voice.

He says nothing.

I ask him if he'd like a drink of something.

No thanks.

He picks up a book, turns it over, reads what it says about the author, and asks, What's it about?

It's a story.

He replaces the book on the shelf and says, Felix likes stories too.

Everyone does, I say.

And afterwards, that's all. I mean, that's really all we are capable of saying. Or doing. Except for one thing. Before he goes, I offer to look after Felix this afternoon if he wants. He says thank you again. Without smiling. I suppose that was what he wanted.

Pierre arrives a little later, with flowers for Maria and flowers for me.

Next comes Jeanne, with Gabriel and Jacques.

We set up the table in the yard and we all eat together. We look like a family in a sequence from an American movie. Friends having a conversation, talking about happy things, but none of them can silence the little suspense they have inside. In the centre of this family the sad little boy has begun to laugh. It's Maria. He can't resist her.

After we've eaten we hear the heavy footsteps again. Felix's father comes in without knocking, he says, Felix?

The little boy gets up quickly, as if he's going to throw himself in his father's arms. He restrains himself. He looks to see if we're watching him. He waves to Maria, then he leaves with his father.

Thanks again.

As soon as the father saw Pierre, he lowered his head. Out of shame. Out of genuine shame.

After they've gone Pierre tells us what he's been keeping to himself since early in the week: he has found a foster family for Felix. The hardest thing is to make himself admit it to him, to Felix. Because children like Felix love their mother and father, he says, more than we can imagine.

Gabriel and Maria will stay up late tonight because it's Saturday. They're sitting on the sofa watching "Pas de pitié pour les croissants." They talk about Salome. Gabriel tells Maria that he used to have an imaginary friend too. That was when I was little, he says.

What was his name?

Pixous.

Did he talk?

Yes. He knew a whole lot of words, like Mummy.

Maria is glad. She goes to get a book from her room and says she has to turn on the night-light for Salome. From there we can hear her telling a story.

Gabriel has come and sat on Jeanne's lap.

It's summer now. We hear children shouting in the lane. Pierre is going to spend the night with me again.

Maria puts on my white T-shirt and moves to the edge of her bed to leave enough room for Salome. Before she falls asleep she says, Mummy there's a lot of people I love, you and Felix and Gabriel and Daddy and Jeanne ... She looks at Pierre and says, You too, but just a little bit. She smiles. It's the kind of smile that means that she loves me more and she will always love me more.

Words

He says, It's a family that has two children already. The parents like to have children, a lot of children, overrun their sunny living room. They know how to live. They explain things. They laugh when one of the youngsters pronounces a word incorrectly.

As for the rest, you never know.

Pierre looks at me. He has been dealing with Felix's case for more than three months now, trying to find a family for him, and everything finally happened so much faster than usual. He looks at me and says, We usually arrive much too late, people clam up, the parents refuse to place their child, or we can't find a foster family, and even when we do, it isn't always better.

He tells me about a little boy who turned himself in to the police yesterday. Eleven years old but he looked no more than eight. Thin, malnourished, covered with bruises. He went there begging to be taken out of his family. At times like that we have no choice, we must move quickly.

The police went to the parents' house right away. They saw what they had to see. There were other children and they were all taken away from the parents that same day. The neighbours remained silent.

In Felix's case too, Pierre sensed that he had to act quickly. At the age of three he hardly talks, he sometimes goes to daycare by himself, he walks with his shoulders hunched like his father's, and there's a nightmare of silence inside him.

Pierre runs his hand over his forehead, he says, Perhaps it's not too late for everything.

On our way home from daycare today we stopped off at Felix's house and dropped a little envelope through the mail slot. Inside it was a pink card with the date and time of Maria's birthday party. We'd also drawn a cake on which Maria had written a four. And of course no candles.

His father saw us from the living-room window, we waited for him to pick up the envelope, open it, give us his answer.

He didn't say anything.

He looked at us, still through the window, and I said, I'll come and pick him up. No need for a present. He nodded.

And then I thought: this may be the last time we see him. I didn't tell Maria that. I thought of his mother whom we hadn't seen since Easter, then of his father who is still there in spite of everything.

Perhaps Felix will be able to come back and live with him one day. It happens sometimes.

And while I was thinking about all that I smiled, because I saw a little boy cross the street, fling open his arms, and hurl himself at his father's stomach. I saw him do that as if it were true, as if it were the only image that could sum up all the desires in the universe today: a little boy being reunited with his father.

2

I pasted into our dream book a photo of Glacier Bay we'd cut from the newspaper just before Easter. It shows some people descending onto the Lamplugh Glacier, one of many in Alaska's Glacier Bay National Park, and it also shows the cruise ship that takes you up the inland passage. Above the picture I printed in capital letters: MARIA AND ALBANIE'S TRIP. It's our birthday present.

It wasn't too complicated, everything was in the article, I mean everything we had to do so we could enter our dream. At the beginning of May I went to the bank and told a man with a wine stain on his tie that I wanted to borrow some money for a sound system. Of course he said yes. Then I bought the plane tickets and I reserved two places on the ship. I put the tickets in the top drawer of my dresser and I didn't say anything to Maria.

This morning she'll find the photo that I've pasted in our book, and her birthday will get underway with a journey to the end of the world. She'll clap her hands, she'll walk up and down in her room, telling the story of her life, and then she'll get into bed with me. And after I've explained it all to her, she'll lie on top of me and snuggle with her head against my neck, because the prospect of being all alone with me in a dream is the best thing about it.

She gets up, finds the photo, and launches into a story with a captain in it. She's telling it to Salome. She's worried because her suitcase is full of Playmobils and there's no room for her clothes. She tells Salome to wait a minute, then she comes to my room to borrow a suitcase. She finds a red one in my closet. She says, Mummy, the marbles are still in your shoe.

She goes to her bedroom, then comes back and asks me if it's her birthday today.

I say, Yes, and it's my birthday too. She thinks about that for a moment and then she starts to sob.

What's wrong, Maria?

She says that there's nobody here, it's not a real party because there aren't any guests.

I tell her to be patient, it's still morning, and besides I've got something to show her.

After I've explained everything she goes to get her book, then she climbs into bed with me. She presses her head against my neck, she says that she loves me and I'll always be her mummy.

It's incredible.

It's incredible that she's four years old today, that this blond little girl snuggling up to me is my little girl and we've been living together for four years. That's why today is not an ordinary day, and why it has to be witnessed by a lot of people. For four years now this little girl has been filling the air with her words, her voice, with her presence that explodes like fireworks. For four years I've been watching her live. And that's what we're going to cele-brate. There won't be even a shadow of sadness in my eyes.

She says auburn. Not blond, Mummy, auburn, like yours. She looks at me reproachfully, as if I'm never pre-cise enough at describing our existence. And then she starts to sing.

We are in my bed, today is Maria's birthday, mine was two days ago but we'll celebrate them together, tonight, and meanwhile this little girl is singing and I am simply there, still astonished at the sight and sound of her.

She is singing. Her memory is more powerful than anything. Even if we've already forgotten certain aspects of these years, this moment is real and startling, it belongs to us.

I will not be sad. The time that is passing will not place its hand over one of my eyes.

3

All at once she stops playing, then turns to me and asks when Daddy will be here. It's not a question but a desire, and she doesn't wait for the answer. Then she rushes at another present, opens it, and discovers Plasticine for making cakes and cookies. She squeals: It's exactly what I wanted!

Our little backyard has been transformed: there are balloons everywhere and two long tables with paper table-cloths. There are crocodiles on them, a jungle, there are even two or three parrots in the distance. Maria doesn't like parrots but they're all right on tablecloths, where they don't make any noise.

In one corner of the yard my father is putting up the swing-set that is his gift to Maria. Pierre goes over to help him. Then Jacques. And finally, Gabriel.

We brought the speakers outside, and right away the children asked for the Pagliaro song they always listen to with the baby-sitter.

Maria asks, What does broken heart mean? and then she wants to know if she's still a little girl, just a bit. I take picture after picture.

I hope one of them will be more extraordinary than the rest, that I'll be able to enlarge it, frame it, put it on my bedroom wall.

She is four years old now, I mustn't forget that, she is four and this is the first time it hasn't rained on her birthday, and she wants to know if she is still a little girl, just a bit. Here in the sun, with her pink sleeveless dress and her white sandals, yes, you're still a little girl, Maria, so little.

Now and then I stand on the steps and watch them all, watch them closely so that nothing escapes me. I'm calmer than I've been other years, I'm getting used to it, I don't see the future in her hair, or in her perfect little shoulders, or in her unfinished sentences.

Felix is here, in fact I think his father has gone to a lot of trouble so he can be here. He's wearing a clean sweater with a teddy bear holding a baseball bat on it, and Maria says he looks cute. We've never seen that expression on his face before.

He's sitting on the grass now, rocking himself and watching the swing-set go up.

Jeanne and I drink a lot and we talk about all the things that have changed over the past year. I think about Maria's father, I miss him today because she does, that's certain.

Jeanne says, Call him. I'm sure he'd be glad to come.

We both look at Pierre and I think, It's her father after all, so I go into the kitchen and phone.

The photo of the three of us is still on the refrigerator, I concentrate on it as I dial his number, and it's focusing on that spot that helps me say, Will you come, it's Maria's birthday.

He says he knows. He was waiting for me to call, like the other times. He misses her. He's glad.

I look out the window at Jeanne explaining something to Pierre. He glances at Maria and smiles.

When we see him come along the lane Maria is so excited that Jeanne and I are sure it was the right thing to do. He kisses her so hard that her cheek is red for a good half-hour.

She drags him to the middle of the yard so he can see the mountain of presents.

A mound, Gabriel corrects her, it's a mound of presents.

Everything is going well. We go on drinking, talking, eating, while the sun sinks quietly behind the house. Now Felix is sitting on one of the swings, Maria is beside him singing *Mahomet* while Gabriel pushes her as high as he can.

There are two cakes, one for the little one, as they say, and one for me, the big one. Mine has thirty-one candles and I blow them out thinking, We must be there, always. On Maria's cake, we've put one candle in the shape of a four, Gabriel blows it out for her, but I'm sure that in her mind there's a tiny little wish. You can see from the way she looks at me. Then she goes and sits on her father's lap and tells him about our trip.

Later, just before she goes to bed, she takes all her toys to her room and deposits them at the foot of her bed, telling me she isn't always sure she's four years old. She means, every minute. She means that sometimes there's an hour in the day when she doesn't feel her age. She says, Sometimes I'm smaller than four. And sometimes I'm bigger. I wrap my arms around her. Me too, Maria.

4

This is a peculiar week.

First of all, when her father left after the party the look on Maria's face divided the air in the backyard into several little compartments. Each person present was enclosed within one of the compartments.

That kind of look always appears after the fact. Maybe she's been marked by it ever since we separated, or maybe she was too young to have such an expression in her eyes before then. I don't know. He finally left saying, See you tomorrow, Maria, because it was Saturday, and she retreated into a corner, angry at me and especially at Pierre.

A few seconds later, of course, it had all been forgotten, but there had been enough time for her gaze to divide the air, to put a little distance between Pierre and me, and to settle into the right hemisphere of my brain.

Every morning over the next few days, she wants to know if she really is four years old now and what does it mean to be four years old. Does it mean to understand and to be able to tie your own shoes? Does it mean to dial Daddy's phone number with no help from anyone? Does it mean not getting into bed with me any more?

She wants to know all that, and she also wants to know the meaning of every new word we use. She's insistent, it doesn't stop. At night she always asks for the same story, the one about the little girl who says goodnight Mummy, goodnight Daddy, and then goes to sleep under a comforter covered with sheep. Occasionally she'll accept something different, but only if it's the book about geometric shapes that Jeanne gave her for her second birthday. I stop at the ends of sentences and let her say the names of the shapes: tent, triangle, cone, balloon, sphere. Ultimately it becomes a kind of prayer that helps us get through the night.

And then there's me, I keep looking out the living-room window because this week Felix is to meet his new family, because that fact is digging a gulf in my heart and

I want to be a witness, once again. To witness what?

Anything at all.

To witness things that are known, betrayed; things unrealized that are floating around us. To be witness to what goes on in other houses, to love, to an event that we think we've forgotten, but that never existed.

The little gulf in the heart beside a story or a word we've never known, causes me—sometimes, often—to look out the window, or to wait for the mailman.

Finally, there is Agnes. She has started really talking to me.

5

It happened on Monday.

In the beginning Agnes would wish me good morning, not with a stiff little nod like Madame Raymond, but a real good morning in a very gentle accent to start the day.

I filed some cards and completed a form for ordering new books. Including one about Alaska. I wasn't looking at Agnes, I had to concentrate very hard because of a kind of discomfort that was caught in my throat. I could see Pierre, I could see the photo on my refrigerator, and I imagined myself stroking Maria's cheek in the picture. Then her father's. And then Maria's again.

I was wondering what we have to do to avoid dragging along with us everybody from our past. But there's one thing: for me, for Maria and her father, the past will never be really past.

Then I went to eat my lunch in the park across from the library, and it was there that Agnes came and sat with me for the first time. She had made some sour cream cakes for my birthday.

I don't know how she found out that I love cakes and cookies made with sour cream, but she knew. She said, laughing, that she was old enough to guess such things. Not the date of my birthday, of course, it was Madame Raymond who told her, when I didn't come to work that day, but the cookies and the tightness in my throat, that she had guessed.

Then we talked about the summer, about my job at the library which I don't like all that much, about Maria, and about her.

She said she'd been watching me for a long time because I reminded her a little of herself when she was younger. A vague smile—that was what she said with her gentle accent.

As for her, she used to work in her father's jewellery store—that wasn't like me—she sold things. She would smile that smile and often look at the clock, like me.

She said she would have liked to have children. When she saw me, she thought about those children, about the garden she'd have made for them every year, about their leaving home, about her loneliness.

But she's not bitter, she said, One should never be bitter.

We talked about a lot of other things and finally, as she got up and brushed off her white skirt with both hands, she said that I was someone she was fond of. She added, That's how it is, and I realized that the tightness in my throat had gone away.

Every day after that she joined me at lunch time.

I finally learned that she came here originally so that she'd feel less alone, that she liked the books and the silence, that she wasn't writing a story, only a letter now

and then, that she wasn't doing anything, that she was agi-
tated enough as it was.

At noon today she took my hand and told me that
she'd spent her youth looking for two people, one who
exists and another who doesn't.

She didn't explain anything, didn't talk about love;
she said, It's time to go back, and, None of that matters
now.

I thought about her all day, and at the end of the afternoon when Maria and I were on our way home we saw
Felix and his father: they were coming back from meeting
the foster family.

I knew today was the day, Pierre had told me, but
because of Agnes's story I'd completely forgotten.

When we saw them I realized right away where they
were coming from.

They were walking in silence, the father holding his
hand for once, and Pierre was on the gallery waiting for us.

6

This peculiar week is ending and now our minds are a little more at ease about Felix.

Everything went very well. During the meeting, Felix
played with a little white cat that is going to make the
connection in his heart. The parents told him its name
was Virgule and he thought that was a very good name. He
smiled when he said that, and things seemed to grow
clearer in his mind.

His father didn't cause any trouble, walled up as he
was in his own helplessness. He gazed at a beam of light
that the sun cast on the floor, he shook the parents' hands.
On the way out, Pierre asked him again where Felix's

mother was, he replied that he didn't know and didn't want to know. He said, She's out of my life.

Now we have to wait. He may agree to be helped and perhaps Felix will be able to come back and live with him again. It will be a long time before we know anything, because today the man is absolutely bereft.

Maria finally understands what it means to be four years old. It was Gabriel who told her.

Being four years old means that next year you won't be going to daycare any more, but to kindergarten. It also means that now you can choose your own clothes in the morning, you can always negotiate, and most important, you can pack your own suitcase when you go to spend a week with your father.

That's what she's doing right now. She tells us that Felix is taking a kind of trip and that she too has to pack her suitcase to go to her father's. Right after breakfast she ran to get the red suitcase from my closet.

I can do it by myself was what she said, just to me. And then that she wasn't leaving me alone on purpose, that it wasn't serious, and that where she was going, to the country, she didn't need her black cat with the bell because she sleeps in the same room as Daddy.

I told her to wait till tomorrow, that it was only Friday. And she said she'd have to think it over, and that it took at least two days to pack a suitcase.

Now she's packing.

Pierre and I watch her, both of us leaning against the door frame. I watch her, I'm happy for her, but at the same time I can't help thinking about Agnes's garden, about her house, about the two people she's been searching for all her life. I think about the gardens of solitude that every one of us invents and I wonder what I'll do for a whole week without Maria.

Pierre says nothing. He knows that I won't take advantage of it as anyone else would, I mean completely. He knows now that there will always be a minuscule Albanie sitting in the middle of Maria's room. He knows my scenarios. It makes no difference to him, what matters is being in love, in as many ways as possible.

When Maria is ready to go to bed, he waits for me in the living room, he doesn't meddle in our life.

He takes a sidelong glance at our family photo on the refrigerator. He tells himself he doesn't see it. That's another scenario.

7

In her suitcase there were two dresses, jewellery, a wallet, a puzzle, and some books. Books I know by heart, she said. She chose them because the source of her greatest pleasure is there, in knowing the whole story by heart, and particularly in feeling the words inside her.

For the rest, I waited till she was asleep and added all the necessary things, even more, needless to say.

She sits on the shore of the lake, her feet trailing in the water, and in front of her, her father is swimming and saying, Come on in, Maria, come in!

She doesn't answer.

She has a new telescope and she's looking at the house across the lake. But if her father swims up to her and holds out his arm she jumps in, and when she's in the water she shivers, throws her head back and shouts, It's cold, it's cold!

At this point I can put someone else in the picture if I want, myself for instance: in one hand I'm holding a hat for Maria, in the other a Campari and soda, and it all exists because there's not a moment's hesitation in our moves.

The images go past very smoothly. It's easy, there's a past and that past contains the lake, the grandparents' house, and a counter that we lean on as we talk and drink our summer drinks. It's so easy that even the words that accompany the images well up in me by themselves, in the same way that the words in Maria's books do for her.

Now Pierre covers my eyes with his hand and suddenly everything disappears, like a drowned body at the bottom of the lake.

This is the first time Pierre and I have been alone together for so long.

In the house I try to occupy the space as if I were twenty years old. I mean, as if there were no past or any of those drowned things at the bottom of a lake.

At times I'm a girl of twenty and Pierre is waiting for me in the evening when I come home from work.

With him the door is always open, I go in, I have an armful of magazines. Pierre is happy that I'm there, he tells me so and then he tells me again, and my work day evaporates on the threshold.

I often talk to him about Agnes. Today she asked about Maria. About her age, her vocabulary, her father. Then she asked about Pierre and again she added that I resemble her.

Now she wears her white skirt almost every day, always carefully ironed. She also wears a multitude of little silver bracelets. She doesn't take them off when she sleeps.

On sunny days, she wears a kind of turban. She is different now, because of the summer.

I know now who David is. Her brother, who disappeared forty years ago, and today is the anniversary of his disappearance. And that's why, after all her questions about me, she told me everything.

David and I, Agnes said, are almost the same age, we're practically twins. One day he left on a trip, and he's never come back. He was twenty, I was nineteen. There was such a strong connection between us that we couldn't name it. And that connection has continued to exist for me, it has continued to make me a woman who was loved, a woman who knows about love and about everything that can be taken away from us. For the first ten years after he disappeared, the image was frozen. We re-read his last letter a thousand times, we wrote to every *poste restante*, we looked for him, and my parents were going out of their minds. They had pinned up his picture in every room in the house. There was David, and what they could imagine about David. Later, they died, and I continued writing to him. But it wasn't about David any more.

Who was it then, Agnes?

I have no idea. Someone I already missed, long before my brother's disappearance, someone I will always miss.

When she said that, I took a good look at her and I understood why she thinks I resemble her. We smiled. Pain is another drowned thing at the bottom of a lake.

Then she told me that she'd been born in the United States, that she'd immigrated here with her family when she was only two years old, she told me about her father's jewellery store, about practically everything.

I came back late from lunch, and all afternoon I could see her, still smiling.

When she left shortly before me, she waved at me and just then, because of her gesture, because of her hand in the air, and her skirt that was a little wrinkled now, I wanted very much to see Pierre, to bring him some maga-zines, to throw myself at him and fuse together in the mid-dle of the living room as if it were a first time. Or a last. It's all the same.

Which was what I did when I walked in the door.

Afterwards, more images of Maria in the country. Images of Agnes too.

Pierre always puts his hand over my eyes when he tries to guess what I'm thinking about. Everything disappears, but never for long.

8

That's it now, Felix has gone.

His father took him to his new home yesterday. The children were playing in the street and the parents greeted him with open arms. Even the little cat was wait-ing in the window. When Felix saw the cat he burst out laughing and he gripped his father's hand more tightly, as tightly as he could.

It was like a party, Pierre keeps telling me. Except for the father of course, and except that Felix didn't under-stand exactly what was going on. Except that he doesn't know that his mother has written, that his father got the letter yesterday morning just before they left. He doesn't know that she won't be coming back, that she's living somewhere out west now, that she wrote on the last line of the paper: I've never felt anything for Felix, that's how it is, I can't do anything about it. He doesn't know and his father will never read that letter to him. He showed it to Pierre and then tore it up in front of him. It was his only witness, the only witness to his life now that Felix isn't there any more.

And I no longer look out the window. If I close my · eyes I can see Felix wearing a little blue beret. It's fall, he is six years old. He's munching a piece of chocolate. He closes his eyes too, and for several seconds he invents his mother's return.

Jeanne left this morning too, for a holiday with Gabriel.

I went over to say goodbye and after the car had turned the corner, Pierre, Jacques and I stayed there saying nothing, the only thing missing was the cloud of dust.

Then Jacques made coffee and told us that things between him and Jeanne were still difficult. By things, he meant love. On the kitchen walls were all the new photos Jeanne had taken during the past months. Jacques was still talking. The photos seemed to have been made for what he was saying.

Then we went out and Pierre hugged me very tight at the corner of the street.

And left me there, because for the first time I was going to visit Agnes at home.

Everything looks just as I'd imagined.

It's an old house on the boulevard. When you go inside there's a smell you can't identify right away.

On the door of her apartment there's a five and when you pull the door shut behind you there is a new smell, sharper, the scent of roses, because there are some in every room.

There's the carpet in the living room, not red but green, an Indian carpet that you immediately want to lie on.

There's a glass-topped table, and on the table a photo album.

Agnes says, Look, that's David.

I don't look. Not yet.

Today she is wearing not her white skirt but a kind of big blue shirt that comes to her knees. She has on white sandals and a white apron where she wipes her hands, which are all stained with strawberries. Her bracelets make less noise here than in the library.

She has been to India, that's clear: the bracelets, the carpet, all that hand-painted cloth on the walls.

She says, Yes, India, Nepal, but that's all in the past.

She opens a bottle of white wine and we sip it slowly, very slowly, while we eat.

She seems at once so contented and so alone, often she seems on the brink of a gesture, a word, but she holds them back. That's what best describes her. On the brink of gestures and words, on the edge of a garden and a solitude all drawn by hand.

Later, after we've eaten, she tells me to look at the photographs. They are important to her. She wants me to see them, to see her and David when they were younger, more in the centre of their lives.

She opens the album and shows me the last page right away. On it are three pictures that Agnes wants to keep in her memory forever.

In the first we see them sitting at the end of a dock, they are small, their four hands hold a fishing-rod. They have taken off their shoes and turned their heads towards the person who has called them.

In the second one they're bigger, they're sitting on a park bench, both of them looking at something in the same newspaper. Beside them on the bench are two open schoolbags and on the ground, a book that has fallen from one of the bags.

Agnes says, It was *Prince Eric*, and I see myself at about the same age, sitting on the floor or on my bed, completely absorbed by the story.

In the third picture we see only David, he's twenty here, he's making a strange sign with his hands. Behind him are tall trees. David too seems very tall. And hand-some. Not altogether present in the picture.

Agnes says, That's one he sent us, from I don't know where. The sign is meant for me, it means I'm thinking about you a lot.

She closes the album and that's all. All for me, not for her.

Then we spend another few moments together in the warmth on the balcony.

9

I didn't tell her about Felix. Or about my visit to Agnes. I didn't tell her that there was something I hadn't imagined, a big white piano against one wall of the living room, and that Agnes had played a very old song on it just for me, a ballad so old that no one knows where it comes from. I didn't tell her because she'll want to go there too, right away. But about Jeanne and Gabriel, I told her everything.

She wants me to tell her the name of the place they've gone to, she repeats it, Bay View, and most of all she wants to know what suitcase Gabriel took.

Suitcases are important. That's what Maria thinks. She

says suitcases and also how many things are in them. How the things are arranged in the suitcase. And what they will bring her.

Then she explains to me that you have to always leave some space free, vacant (though that's not the word she uses) in the suitcase. That place is where the treasure will be found, a seashell or some other souvenir; it's the place where desire will be found.

She shows me the treasure in *her* suitcase. It's a drawing for me. It shows a house on pilings and underneath it, she says, is the river. She has added three cliffs, the sun, some birds because I showed her how to draw them, and a little girl in the river. She has written her name, Maria, with two capital As.

Do you like it, Mummy?

Yes, Maria, it's the most beautiful drawing I've ever seen.

Today is Sunday, Maria's suitcase day. Her father asks me if he can stay for a while, of course, it's always hard to cross the threshold. Especially when you have to leave Maria behind. Especially after a whole week with her.

She doesn't ask where Pierre is, she's forgotten all about him for the moment. So have I for that matter, but it's all right, because love is something that invents itself.

And so, standing there in front of me, Maria's father is as tall and handsome as David was in front of the trees, and he's in the process of inventing something. Perhaps it has something to do with the past, because the past is always present here on the refrigerator door. And perhaps it has something to do with his loneliness as well. And what is it that touches his solitude most at this moment if not the two of us, Maria and I, sitting on her bed, unpacking her suitcase, and sometimes looking at him and laughing?

He doesn't say anything, but I know what he is think-ing. I mean, I can guess at the shape of his thoughts. And that shape contains not him and me but Maria and me, and this whole life that's continuing.

Later I tell him, It's really time to go now, because we're leaving too. Maria wants to see Grandpa's birds again.

She gives him lots of kisses on his neck, then she shouts Bye, bye as she runs ahead of me.

He rolls down the car window, he says I look beautiful today.

It's nothing, not even the image of his own desire.

10

The song that Agnes played for me is still in my head. Even Maria can hum it. It goes with us everywhere. Agnes says it should go with us on our trip.

Now there's a postcard on the refrigerator door, with two lobsters on it: Jeanne and Gabriel. On the back they've simply written, Look at us! and from the way they've written the letters we can see them there, lying in the sand.

While we wait for them to come home, it's our turn to get ready for our trip. We've started making lists. Sometimes Pierre helps us. My mother has bought a suit-case just for Maria. And at lunch time Agnes tells me sto-ries about boats.

I have said that love is something that invents itself. For instance, you can fall madly in love while listening to the latest record by The Blue Nile. It can last for an evening, a night, a week, until a war breaks out or a window is shattered or nothing at all, until you don't have enough time to think about it any more.

I listen to The Blue Nile by myself sometimes, standing in the middle of the living room. Which means precisely: in the middle of the house. And every time, I fall in love all by myself, I think about Pierre because he's there, because it's through him that love has come alive again. Which means precisely that a person's chief quality, a person's greatest chance, is to be there. To be there entirely. And all of us must demonstrate our presence on earth in one way or another. Agnes has spent a good part of her life looking for her brother: that demonstrates her presence on earth. She is searching. His love always comes back towards her. It's painful, but it's a kind of happiness too. The same for Jeanne. And for me. For everyone.

Yesterday, I took Maria with me to visit Agnes. The three of us sat on the balcony, it was late afternoon and Maria said, In summer the nighttime is different, it isn't really night.

She never stopped talking. She named everything she saw: the smoke from a distant incinerator, dogs, bicycles, people coming home from work, rolling up their sleeves and watering their gardens. She talked and talked and Agnes was amazed.

We stayed to have something to drink and Maria began to make up stories about Felix. It was the first time she'd mentioned him since he went away. So I told her that he was in his new house now and she said she knew. I don't know how, but she knew.

Finally, Agnes walked us to the corner of the street and there she said, I'm not alone any more. Into Maria's ear she

added, I have two friends, she bent over her and her pos-
ture cast a strange shadow on her smile. On Maria's mouth.

In my heart it created a weight, a very small one, but
still a weight, a heaviness, like a stone thrown into the sky.

11

In the summer it's as if a swamp is slowly forming where
the daycare is. In the middle of it sits the school, it's an
eddy and you never know what you're about to dive into,
or who will be there to greet you. In the morning you get
dressed, you say something a little absent-mindedly, sometimes totally dazed, you leave the house with great lightness, it's summer, the air is filled with us, the surfaces are
calm, and it lasts until we arrive there.

Then we climb the stairs and as soon as we open the
door, everything starts to disperse.

Take this morning, for instance.

We enter the swamp, it's warm, it's as if we're removed
from something, but until then it's normal.

There's the corridor and at the end of it, Maria's classroom.

There's no one in the classroom.

We go back in the opposite direction, we look for the
children, Maria's getting upset. She should be, I'm upset
too. She tells me we can't find her group and I don't like
that, a four-year-old who has lost her group and is wiping
sweat off her forehead like an old lady.

Finally we find a classroom full of children, and a
teacher I don't know who says, There's no room for Maria
here, everything is complicated today, go and try another
class. At that, of course, Maria starts to cry.

It can't be. For a few seconds, everything going on in

my thirty-one-year-old head is like a four-year-old's nightmare.

I tell Maria, Come on, we're going. I take her hand, then we leave and go back to the house.

Later, I call Madame Raymond to explain why I'm not at work today. She replies, as if it's been prepared in advance, This is the last time, Albanie.

I'm not afraid of her.

What frightens me now is not the swamp or the school or the eddy that to some degree I've created: it's the weight of a body in a river. The body has come up to the surface, to the shore, and then to us.

The body is that of Felix's father, he threw it into the river.

When Pierre arrived just now to tell me, he took the newspaper from his bag and I saw the name, the name of Felix's father, his name was Jean, I knew it but I realized I'd never asked him what his name was, I'd never called him by that name. I also thought about Maria's father.

After that I didn't know what to say because Pierre was crying, his head on the table, and a moment later the question hit us like a bomb. How would we tell Felix? How would we tell him he had lost his father and his mother and that for the rest of his life he would never know why?

Maria is asleep now, Pierre is still hunched over the table and the drowned man's body frightens me. All drowned bodies frighten me, but this one even more. Because his name is Jean, a name that is so real. Because he loved that woman who went away, and because he didn't know what to do after she'd gone. It's as if he was no better off where he is now, he's still breathing, just enough for the six-year-old Felix to walk past me one more time. He doesn't eat chocolate any more, he says things from before his time, he speaks sentences of which he has no knowledge.

The whole story is in the newspaper. The story of the separation. We don't know who told it. There are the names of witnesses. Assumptions. Fortunately, Felix's name isn't there. We don't know everything. All we know for certain is that the body had been there for several days, that it took several days to come back upstream to us.

The paper lies open on the table. Pierre doesn't move. He has to think, but that is always accompanied by a certain pain, by what refuses to be thought. Often, we don't know what's stopping us from going further. I mean, in our thinking. This time though everything is clear, we know what will be wrong in the future, in the present, even what was done badly in the past.

That's why Pierre doesn't move. He sits there over the open newspaper all night, to discover what he knows about this drowned body.

Over the next few days we talk about nothing else. Especially Pierre, he keeps coming back to it.

We have closed the newspaper and thrown it into a green bag with the remains of supper, but nothing helps, we keep seeing the grey photo of the body that was fished out of the water, it's there between us.

We haven't said anything to Maria.

The next day Pierre went to Felix's new family and the parents assured him that they'd look after everything, they'd tell Felix in their own words, with their own silence and Felix's, when the time came. And when the time comes Pierre will see to the adoption. For that, he'll have to find the mother and he's already started the research.

Pierre liked the foster parents very much that morning. They were together in the kitchen, there was something gentle in their eyes. Exactly like Pierre. Felix was sitting on the floor with the little cat, now and then the father would run his fingers through the boy's hair, he would bow his head, and altogether it formed a calming tableau.

And then Pierre continued to love me. All week, he loved me a little harder than usual.

12

They're home!

They just stopped at their house to drop off their baggage and now they're here at our door, all tanned and with reddish highlights in their hair.

Jeanne is wearing dark glasses like Jackie Onassis. Gabriel is holding her hand and Maria sees the little white line on his wrist right away. That's from my watch, he says, it got lost in the ocean.

We don't say anything to Jeanne about what happened; now she's telling us about the house she rented, about the sand-castles they built, the California wines she drank, about the sea, the sea that is a different colour every day and that every day returns us to ourselves.

Jeanne laughs. She sets us ablaze with her laughter. Jacques is beside her, and for once they are truly happy to be together. I mean, simply happy. Ordinary. Like someone who has missed another person and who has no words hidden in his pockets.

In two days it will be our turn to go away. Our bags are already packed and the more Jeanne talks, the more eager I am, the more I picture Maria's little face at the window, above the wing of the airplane.

Will things really be resolved when we come home? In the life of Felix? Of Agnes?

A year has just passed over the bodies of several persons, but that doesn't tell us anything about the future. For me, only one thing is certain: there will always be someone or something along my way, wherever I am, to give me an image of my life. Look, there it is: the hidden shoes, the strange light on the floor, the houses, Agnes, the glaciers, Maria and the quaking earth ... It's Albanie!

At the beginning of this year there was our dream book, and at the end there will be our travel book. In the beginning, words, and at the end, more words. That's how we come closer and closer to what we are. And perhaps that's how things will continue to be?

Agnes thinks so. A while ago she asked me to write about our trip, and as she asked she gave me a one-hundred-and-ninety-two page pink Clairefontaine notebook. I said, That's too much, and she replied, Nothing is ever too much. I meant the number of pages, while she meant life, or love, or everything that flows between people.

Then she held out something even stranger: an envelope containing a rather large sum of money and David's photograph. She said, The money is to help pay for your trip. I said no. That I'd already borrowed what I needed and I didn't care if it took five years to pay it back. She said, It's not that. She looked at the picture of David, and the only thing I could think of to say was, He's dead, Agnes. She said again, It's not that, and then I saw in her eyes that I couldn't refuse. It was an order. A mild and desperate order. An order connected to the past. I thought of what Jeanne always says: life is a movie and in that movie there's a relay race. I took the picture of David and it burned my hands like a torch. I took the torch, it's mine now, and I pressed it to my chest. It burned me again but it doesn't matter, because in that place there are so many other burns.

But now I don't know if I should keep it.

That's what I tell Jeanne and we burst out laughing because we're both thinking exactly the same thing. We look at the diamond she's wearing again, we look at Jacques, then at Pierre and Gabriel and Maria, and finally Jeanne says, We can't do anything about it. Saying that, she makes the same gesture as Agnes, she means our lives, our heads, and our desires that change and don't change.

Then Maria asks Gabriel if there are dogs by the ocean and if there are any in Alaska. When he says yes, she thinks as she searches for the most appropriate word in her private dictionary, and the word she settles on is "unfair": she says, It's unfair that there are dogs. Her face is impossible and I'm sure she can see, as I do, drooling dogs that stand at street corners, waiting. There are also groups of people at the ends of the lanes, parents who let their children go to their first day of school by themselves. There is a drowned body and the body of a brother who has disappeared. And that's nothing. There's much more still. For the moment though there are the dogs; with Maria we always come back to dogs.

Gabriel says there were lots of dogs at the ocean and he's not afraid of them.

Jeanne smiles: what he's afraid of is the water. The images of that fear of his gather by themselves, they are already memories that surround Jeanne. Already they recognize our voices. Each of us adds something to it until the moment when Jeanne asks: What about Felix?

We pick up the bottle of rum, we fill our glasses, and it's Maria who replies.

13

What I haven't yet mentioned about Maria is the way she interferes in conversations. She always alights beside us in one way or another, at top speed, she listens without seeming to, and she talks a mile a minute.

That's because Maria understands everything. When I say everything I mean everything, really everything. She would understand even if we were speaking another language.

Whenever Pierre and I are discussing something, whenever we're sure she's not listening, whenever we forget about her even briefly, we're wrong, she's right there. It's when we're inattentive that she understands best. She's there and her presence is enough. And sooner or later our phrases come back to us, they spring to life again with new contents, with connections that only Maria has been able to make.

When Jeanne asked about Felix, she replied: His father died in the ocean. She didn't say he fell, she invented a wharf, the pitch-black night, fish. Gabriel listened, he was in the process of composing his own version of things.

She said, Mummy knows what it said in the paper. Adding, It's not for children.

She knows everything. That's what I told Jeanne. She knows everything and I'll stay close to her all my life, I'll carry her on my back or in my arms as I did at the very beginning, and through her I too will have the knowledge she possesses of what it is we desire, what we want to be.

Of course we still had to explain it all to Jeanne and Jacques. It wasn't the ocean, but the river. His body plunged into the blackness.

Our eyes, Pierre's and mine, filled with tears, and at the end Maria said, now he's a real orphan, like Salome.

She went to her room, she told Gabriel, Come on, let's console my imaginary little sister.

The next day, with Maria gone to spend the day at her father's, Pierre and I decide to drive past Felix's house. His house?

We want to see. To see what? We don't know, but we want to look through the keyhole for a while, just for a while. We need to.

There's a little white wrought-iron fence, the grass needs cutting, it's full of dandelions, the gate is open, and suddenly we spy Felix holding Virgule in his arms.

He comes outside. Like all children, he has the sun in his hair.

He walks down the three steps. He turns around because another little boy has come up behind him with a ball.

He doesn't say anything.

He looks down at the ground.

He sets the cat down at his feet and smiles at it, then he sits down to tie the shoelace that has come undone.

We can see him very clearly. His shoes are brand-new, red, and the laces are incredibly white.

The other little boy helps him tie a bow. Then they both get up and start playing with the ball.

14

Saturday. Departure day.

Agnes came over last night with a tape that she made just for us. For Albanie and Maria. It's the old song she played for us on the piano.

I said, Thank you, Agnes, thank you for everything,

and I kissed her, leaving a nice lipstick mark on her cheek.

She wanted to see Maria, but Maria wasn't there. She had stayed overnight at her father's.

He'll be here in a while to take us to the airport, that's what they decided. I couldn't say no. Pierre even less.

Before I went to bed I played the tape on my Walkman to see how it sounded. It sounded, all right! I was a little dazed because of the rum we'd drunk, for dessert this time, with just some little ice cubes, and finally I couldn't get to sleep.

I got up in the middle of the night to copy something from *The Member of the Wedding*, which I'd been carrying in my purse since my last day at work.

She said again:

"Luxembourg. Don't you think that's a lovely name?"

Berenice roused herself. "Well, Baby—it brings to my mind soapy water. But it's a kind of pretty name."

"There is a basement in the new house. And a laundry room." She added, after a minute, "We will most likely pass through Luxembourg when we go around the world together."

And that's the end of the story of Frankie Addams. Just before the silence is shattered and she hears *with an instant shock of happiness* the ringing of the bell.

I put that text on the refrigerator door in place of the old one, and this morning when Pierre came to join me in the kitchen, I told him, Those words will inhabit the house while we're away.

Pierre looked at me for a long time. Then he said, Those sentences are too long, Albanie. He took the photo of the three of us, me, Maria, and her father, he dropped it into the basket above the fridge, then he put the pink paper with the text on it in the middle of the freezer door. There, he said, that's better.

Later, after breakfast, he looked at me for a long time again, like in a movie in which there are two people, one of them with a suitcase, and he said, I love you, Albanie.

The way he said it immediately placed me at the centre of the universe.

I understand now. I understand why I love him too. And why I love Jeanne and Agnes. Because our way of loving contains love, of course, but it also contains Felix, his father's suicide, abandonment, worry, murder everywhere. When Pierre says he loves me, I know that behind his words there's a vacant lot filled with desolation. The world is like that, desolate, like a gas station in the American desert.

Any minute now Maria will arrive with her father, I'll take her in my arms, I'll love her, and the desolate world will go and stretch out in what remains of the sky. She'll be wearing her sleeveless pink dress, she'll have little ponytails tied with ribbons, her heart will beat too hard, much too hard for such a little girl. And that will last all her life.

We are about to enter our year-long dream, then we'll leave it. Later we may enter another dream and the space in our bodies will expand. In the end, we'll emerge from it. But nothing inside will ever be peaceful again.

Life is something stolen, we don't know why. One day our trip will be forgotten. Our postcards vanished. And then us. We don't know why.

For the moment though, Pierre has already gone and I'm all alone in the backyard. I'm ready. I'm waiting.

I put the notebook from Agnes in a little bag that I'll keep with me during the trip. It also holds candies for Maria, her book about ships, her sunglasses, lipstick, a mirror, and some little things for Salome.

I'm ready. Waiting.

When I close my eyes I see a freight train, it's travelling too fast, nothing is fastened down, everything comes loose and falls off the sides. Boxes, chains, food, treasures, everything. In the end, someone steps out of an empty car and goes onto a deserted beach to fill a notebook.

That is our journey.

And perhaps one day we'll all be on that beach, our hearts at once a little lighter and a little heavier, all joined together by an invisible thread.

A dream.

I open my eyes and my dream is suspended, because a little voice is asking if I'm ready. It's Maria. Her heart is beating too fast.

She says, Are you coming? and we go on our way in a *shock of happiness.*

Élise Turcotte was born in Sorel, Quebec, in 1957, and studied French literature at the Universitié du Québec à Montréal. She a is well-known poet and two-time winner of the Prix Émile-Nelligan. *The Sound of Living Things* is her first novel.

Sheila Fischman is the award-winning translator of more than fifty novels from Quebec. She lives in Montreal.

Coach House Press
50 Prince Arthur Avenue, Suite 107
Toronto, Canada M5R 1B5

Cover Design: Shari Spier / Reactor
Cover Illustration: *Sans Titre* by Jacques Payette,
Private collection.
Reproduced by permission of
Michel Tétreault Art International,
Montreal.